DIRTY SAINTS

Sobek Khaskhemwy Meri Ra

SOBEK KHASKHEMWY MERI RA

Books may be purchased in quantity and/or special sales by contacting the publisher Dzifa Publishing at 424-242-5431 or tasenetmerira@gmail.com.

Published by Dzifa Publishing
Interior Design by DeVondia Roseborough
Cover Design by Dynasty's Cover Me
Editing by Sobek Kaskhemwy Meri Ra
ISBN: ISBN 978-0-578-66907-6
First Edition

Printed in USA

DEDICATIONS TO THE ONES I LOVE

This book is dedicated to Ann Bynum my… LIVING mother, who did her best to protect me from the world that I had to jump into. I LOVE YOU MAMA, don't ever fucking forget that.

This book is dedicated to those who have survived trauma in their life, who carried the shame and fought within themselves to FULLY commit to NOT crossing the line of "the point of no return".

To those who fight and win within themselves, the daily battle in the war for their soul to be clean.
This book is dedicated to those who have committed sins in their past, who walk the "lone road of redemption" in a world that speak of a forgiveness, yet offer none.

Judging those who openly admit their offenses, while hiding their sins.
This book is dedicated to the Dirty Saints in the REAL world…. I got you

Sobek Khaskhemwy Meri Ra

SOBEK KHASKHEMWY MERI RA

CHAPTER 1

"Man, it's cold as fuck! I wish this chick would come on. I am sitting here freezing my ass off, this bench sure ain't no heating pad." It is one of the coldest nights during the Christmas holidays. Crowds of people mostly from the suburbs are shopping downtown on State Street and Michigan Ave. The decorations in Bloomingdales, Salvation Army's Santa's lining the sidewalks and the business people traveling the traditional ways of welcoming St. Nick, buying expensive gifts. This is the picture of the holiday spirit in Chicago. Michael Lee is sitting in Washington Park, keeping himself company among the old concrete statues of Chicago's sons of Liberty. The statues of old white men and the written history of their lies. The real story is that this city was actually founded by a black man named Jean Baptiste Point du Sable, a Haitian National. Silence has its own sound, like a calling for eternity to make its presence known. This past week of snow brings forth a blanket of calm before chaos lets its children loose on humankind.

SOBEK KHASKHEMWY MERI RA

This is theuniverse's much-appreciated moment of silence however brief. Michael Lee sees the frozen Great Lake Michigan, witnessing the path where shadows leave footprints walking to an unknown destination. The breeze off the Great Lake is the infamous "hawk" that the city of Chicago is known for. It is said that if you are not from the city of Chicago, it will let you know you are in the Windy City.

"It's cold da thana motherfucka out here. I'm glad that I am wearing these long johns momma got me with a pair of heavy-duty thick socks…momma always on time. It helps being in this cold ass snow when wanting to be somewhere else." The black navy coat of heavy wool is armor against the wind over a heavy-duty black hoodie. His stressed- jeans revealed black long johns, along with a turtleneck, gloves, black construction boots, a wool scarf wrapped and draped lopsided on the front. The all black ensemble acts as a dot in the midst of untouched virgin white snow of Chicago's Eastside wonderland. In the withering light of a straining lamppost struggling under the weight of the snow, emerges a distinct silhouette. Michael keeping a relaxed and even tone, camouflages his agitation for the long wait. "Ya know, I wish folks would comprehend that keeping people waiting is not cool, civilized folk like yourself would call that being, rude" Michael said.

From out of the edge of the darkness, as the fresh snow slightly moans feeling the weight of her boots, a very elegant mysterious silhouette takes form.

A commanding sultry voice offers a reply, "My dear Michael Lee I apologize for the wait, I lost track of time dealing with some very weak-minded creatures. You men are never satisfied. The meeting this evening with our allies went a little longer than it should. They needed some assurances for me not to destroy their Houses and I needed a little more convincing. They did betray my trust, so I used the opportunity to watch them plead their cases. The joy of watching them beg… it was priceless."

Cleopatra Rex, the keeper of Hell's Stone Manor and Baroness of Hannibal Guild, quietly appears in the spaces of the flickering light of the lamppost. The vision is flawless black Abyssinian skin, black onyx locs long and flowing, and seductive almond shaped-eyes. Her cold calculating presence is BEAUTIFULLY DANGEROUS. In the beginning of her reign as Baroness was as a crucible of living up to the reputation of her father. Her ruthless intelligence exceeded all her siblings, even her uncle Bilal. Smiling, Michael lifts himself off the back of the park bench shaking the snow off his gloves. While Cleopatra patiently waits wearing her deep red fur coat, black leather jumpsuit, and high-end boots with the skinniest of stiletto heels. Cleopatra senses Michael Lee's effort as he walks toward her, "You are holding your temper very well Michael,

I applaud this civility" she said. Michael Lee continues to calmly approach, stopping just in front of her, the smile slowly dissipates from his face.

"Thanks for noticing my improvement in manners, I just need information. Give me a name and crew, since you are giving me and this situation your valuable attention" Michael said. The recent murders happening on the Belmont Rocks is a real ugly scene now.

Looking at the lake it brings me a sort of peace. "The peace that I need in this life I live" ... pausing in reflection, "This is…. my favorite space. It was better than being where I lived, going there to get away from the 'Hood."

Cleopatra steps closer to Michael Lee, "That is so admirable of you, shows you have some human decency, some kindness left in you. So, let me ask you a question, you think this could lead you to my brother? I need to make sure that you are not hiding emotions that can bring failure. It would not be good for either one of us, for me it's business and for you it's getting to my disgrace of a brother," she said. Reaching in his left coat pocket pulling out a lighter, his right hand reaches into his left breast pocket coming out with a fat and perfectly rolled blunt.

"Baroness, I let that comment slide, I hooked up with you to get rid of some of your associates and that is what I do. Ever since I got this mark of the Seal of Set on my chest, the past 2 years have been different. Killing demons, seeing other types of spirits. Shit you read in the Bible and comic books, yes, I can get a little zealous in doing it. I am not going to trip or go crazy, but I'm gonna let you know on tha' real.... after this is done it's back to business as usual" Michael said. Cleopatra knew he was after her brother Apas. That was the reason for her late arrival; she received news she was receiving from her spy guild. Mephisto Lynx, the Lord of Sheol House, was behind a lot more than the murders at the Belmont Rocks.

"You are looking for Montello Roy and his crew, they are seeking to control the Uptown area. A pack of hungry wolves, who want to run the heroin and cocaine connection, they are just small timers. The murders are a message to everyone to make their presence known. In addition to gaining an audience with Keon Lynx and Sheol House who runs all the Near North Side to all of Roger's Park."

Cleopatra loudly sighs, "They can have all that area, it's way too BORING for me. I prefer the South Side; profit is better along with the West and East side. Another thing every Fallen and human ally knows about you Michael Lee; the one who kills Elite Fallen. I advise you to bring your best game... those boys are dying for a piece of you. They're wanting the fame of killing the one endowed with the Seal of Set. You killed Barabasi when no one else could, knowing that, be a good boy and kindly slaughter each and every one of them." As she begins to walk past him, he clasps her wrist ever so slightly, leans in close to her ear and whispers. "I would be glad to wipe those motherfuckas off the face of the earth. Then I am coming for your punk ass brother." Smiling, however, sinister yet seductively she replies, "I will gladly assist you in any way I can, I look forward to that." Walking away with the Unseen, she disappears from Michael Lee's sight fading into the blackness of night. With her are the Unseen, beings of immense power. Loyal only to the Hannibal Guild and known for their many victories in battle. As they approach the limo one moves swiftly to open the back-passenger door, the other continues on to the driver's side getting in. Before getting in herself, "One more thing Michael, your sister is alive." She smiles at the expression on his face, leaving Michael Lee staring, as the rear lights exit out of Washington Park. Michael Lee thought to himself, "One day baby girl me and you are going all out, the gods aint gonna have nothing to say when I am done."

As he leaves his lone footsteps are the story of a meeting between enemies forced to be allies. Michael Lee's sister disappearance two years ago brought him to accept the responsibility of The Seal of Set. The feelings of vengeance and the rage towards everything in life was now released and focused. Every Fallen he encountered was mercilessly slaughtered without discrimination. Living that dog eat dog street life, a world of fighting for everything fueling his mind. In this early period of killing Fallen while still in the Game his soul evolved to much darker levels. He was believed to be a human having the soul of a Fallen. Had it not been for the love of his sister, who kept him in touch with the good in him, that acts as a reminder that he must always stay on his square. He feels the world wouldn't miss a person like her even though this world needed more people like her. Fallen and other beings of Hades Realm wouldn't want someone like her in this world. It doesn't fuckin matter to him, he blames the gods and Fallen alike, they're ALL going to pay.

CHAPTER 2

Back then Cleopatra was not especially fond of Apas, an intense sibling rivalry that borderlines hate. Everything was given to both of them, they wanted for nothing and yet SHE wanted more. What she wanted was simple and that is to rule Hannibal Guild, not to just be a lady in court. Her resolve was absolute, in her mind her brothers will always be second to her. A resolve that comes from a life of privilege and traditions being that she was no one important and her duty was only to marry into human high society. It seemed to her that Fallen and humans alike have the same mundane traditions… of bringing wealth and expanding power. Her brother's disappearance six years ago sparked the minds of the Hannibal Guild's High Council; they assumed she was responsible. Laughing out loud proclaiming, "They are just mad because they can't fuck me, the nerve of them limp dick assholes. Always kissing up to Father, while planning to stab him in the back. They have yet begun to pay for their fucking hypocrisy. I am going to destroy their reputations, their power and influence. I am going to slaughter all of them, including their families!" Cleopatra said. Four years ago, her father was assassinated, stabbed in the heart. The fatal wound was said to be made by the sword known as the Black Purge. A weapon that is thought to be in the Vault of Apep in the city of Ambrose, located in the Otherworld. His body was found in his inner-chamber, his bed soaked in black blood. Cleopatra used the opportunity to seize power. During this time Hannibal Guild was at war with the House of Darius. She had decided to decimate the House of Darius, a sworn enemy. Despite the High Council's tradition of the eldest male figure being ordained Baron, that would be her first cousin Lexus. She got the support of other Lords and began to wage war on the House of Darius and other enemies. Her talents as a strategist and tactician are precise and deadly. Commanding the highest form of psychological warfare and industrial espionage makes her a worthy adversary to Fallen and human. In two years, the House of Darius became an ally, rather a foot stool. An elite force was formed from loyal families that were loyal to her father, who are now loyal to her. High ranking officers, their subordinates and specialists came under her rule, now known as The Network. Targeting ALL enemies present and past including their extended families. Their reputation precedes them where no one talks openly about them. Their exploits are compared to nightmares, those who are released are not the same. As she travels deeper into her memories, she smiles looking at the moon in the night frigid sky. Cleopatra fully relaxes into the soft leather of the limo's back seat. Reflecting on her rise to power brings her elation, she orders her bodyguard.

"Pour me a glass of Shiraz, I want to celebrate this moment. My biggest threat has become my most important "ally" Her personal creed has been and always will be that **"rule all and those who oppose destroy."** In her bloodline she is the FIRST female to rule and she is moving to be the most feared. Her ascension has never been opposed, her reputation never to be questioned, she is known to be unpredictable and merciless. In her dark heart she understands the feeling of Michael Lee's resolve and she can see that he has never been one to feign purity. She despises posed purity, humans and Fallen alike, particular humans who she felt did not understand the full scope of their choices. Cleo felt that humans took their free agency for granted, free will was a waste on them. The one thing she does know is that Michael Lee is committed to the absolute destruction of those Fallen in this city. He is not the type of human who goes about pretending to be pure or innocent. She sees the heart of a Dark Son, yet holding back that immense power. He has not fully realized himself after having killed a Dark Elite. Having been stained with the blood of such a powerful and ancient one...he survived. This human being has ignited a fascination and interest, feelings of wanting to be near him. To be a witness of the battle he fights within himself, the powers of Hades Realm and Celestial Atum within him. His resonance is fueled with the power of true choice, accepting the responsibility of the Seal of Set. She wonders how he fights his own soul's dreadfulness, contemplating that it's something that ALL humans share. What motivates them to do the inhuman things they do? Michael Lee is a living testament to having embraced his dark nature. Instead of running from it, he chooses to live without apology. The dark never had to chase him… he simply walks in it. She continues to ponder staying lost in thought, she smiles at her reflection looking out the window.

"So peaceful is the city without the scurry of humans, ruining my view,"

Cleopatra muses out loud. The driver looking into the rear-view mirror smiles, revealing fangs behind a human facade agreeing with his Mistress's opinion.

"I am hungry Simi; I would like to dine in at home tonight. Call Bishop to wake the chef, I am in the mood for Filet Mignon."

Simi replies, "As you wish my Baroness." The limo picking up speed traveling the vacant avenue.

CHAPTER 3

The news of his sister being alive has done more than stun him; he stands frozen long after Cleopatra's departure. Realizing that the snow begins to fall again, he allows it to fall in his hand. Watching as it melts into his palm staring into the empty palm, taking in a deep breath he reaches for his cell phone. Pushing the speed dial a few times, there is a click, "Yo, I just met with Cleopatra and you were on the money about the name."

No reply from the other end, he waits a little longer. "Say something Cuz, just don't talk shit, I'm a little bugged right now." Loud laughter comes into the quiet night, Sol begins to snicker.

"Brother, you know I am going to talk some shit, because that's what I do. I told your stubborn ass in the first place that my sources are good. I got eyes and ears everywhere, why you think I am always right. I am the "eyes" of the Southside of The Chi."

"I knew it was Montello Roy and his crew, they are making their move to tap in the Northside underground action. They make their Ends from selling drugs to those gay dudes in Boys Town. Also, you are right that Cleopatra wasn't going to tell me that Toni Ann was kidnapped." Sol is Michael Lee's right-hand man, the voice of reason. Sol has known Michael Lee since they were kids; they grew up on the block together in the neighborhood. He is the brother that Michael Lee never had and one of the few in his inner circle. The moments when Michael Lee phases out Sol has been there, counseling him on what is REAL during those P.T.S.D. episodes. Sol was there that Halloween night two years ago when Michael Lee received The Seal of Set. That was also the night Michael Lee saved his life. Sol has that talent, that gift of discernment, that feeling before shit happens.

Sol's voice brings Michael Lee back to the present, "I know you are trying not to laugh. We have been doing this long enough to know when the game is being run; **'game peep game'**, so stop trippin."

"Don't have me come to your crib to spank you in front of Shammi. Give Ty and Cyril a ring. Those two are probably over some chick's crib, blowing trees and trying to talk philosophy shit. I'm heading to your spot. I got a plan to fuck up Montello's mix, this cat is about to see how much I make Fallen bleed. He's about to find that out with tha quickness. This is one of the reasons I am involving us in this situation, one more thing Toni Ann is alive, I just found out and I don't know how to feel, that's

SOBEK KHASKHEMWY MERI RA

why I am glad you are rolling with me on this demonstration. I'll see you and Shammi when I get there. I gotta drive in this snow, you know how people drive in this shit, ya feel me? Later man…. peace." Michael Lee hangs up and sighs, "I am coming to get you Sis, sit tight."

CHAPTER 4

It's 6 a.m. and Montello Roy, head of the Ajax Clan sits in his downtown office. Walls are lined with encased newspaper headlines of recorded major events that have changed the world. He reflects on these memories; these moments of time are the staples of his motivations for the power play he is orchestrating. With simmering hate and loathing directed towards the one clan he wishes to destroy; Hannibal Guild is at the top of the list. He feels that the Guild looks down on all of the Fallen clans including his. Every headline on the wall is connected to the Hannibal Guild behind the scenes, from the Stock Market crash in New York to the Valentine Day's Massacre right here in Chicago's Lincoln Park that same year in 1929. Ajax's father told him stories of Hannibal Guild's control of the Catholic Church and The Spanish Inquisition of the Dark Ages. The guild had control of King Ferdinand and Queen Isabella of Spain, under the guise to unite Spain and the Catholic Church. Responsible for the torture and murder of innocent people who would not join the Catholic Church. Those who have been a threat or opposed their power have been dealt with in grand and open fashion. Clandestine control in the election of certain politicians in the City of Chicago, even the power of the President of the United States. They were behind Al Capone and the rest of the Cosa Nostra who was running things here in Chicago. Hannibal Guild funded the mafia criminal operations from the East Coast to the casinos in Las Vegas, every mayor of Chicago has answered to them, even today. They are rumors that they were responsible for the Great Chicago Fire of 1871. Two days the city burned over 300 people were killed and 100,000 people lost their homes, a full three-square block burned. The objective was to gain cheap real estate for legit businesses working as a cover for their criminal operations in Chicago. This provided funds to finance Hannibal Guild's operations in Chicago and the Global Black Market. Hannibal Guild with its power and influence has been in Chicago for centuries. Chicago is the place they call home. Montello was caught in the trance of paperwork on his desk, he didn't feel the presence of Sheikh James. Sheikh James stood 6' 11" bald, dark complexion and muscular, he quietly entered Montello's office. Sheikh's aura has a strength that would lead people to think of someone who is head of security for Montello. The role of being Montello's Director of Operations of Roy Enterprises fits him as well. Roy Enterprises is the conglomerate of real estate, sports management and retail, that finance Montello's growing criminal endeavors. Sheikh is the mind and force behind ALL that goes on. He makes up for what Montello's business sense misses, which is a strong grasp of common sense. In other words, Sheikh is the quintessential man behind the scenes.

A soft spoken and deep voice, "Montello it's time." Resonates with Montello, bringing him back to the real world.

"Sir, Keon Lynx is sitting in the living room waiting." Montello regains his composure, stands up and adjusts himself. Sheikh opens the closet door removing the freshly pressed suit jacket from its wooden hanger. Montello grabs the jacket slowly and gently moves while putting it on, he does a final check in the nearby mirror. He wants the appearance of power and control, he smiles in satisfaction and confidence. He walks out his office down the hall towards the living room. Sheikh, who is joined by two of his staff, follows him closely behind. As he casually strolls, he sets his mind on the meeting with Keon Lynx the Viceroy of Sheol House.   As Montello enters the foyer, he first glances at the heavily muscled bodyguard positioned near the private elevator at the entry to the condominium. Walking past the bodyguard Sheikh's staff takes position at the end of the foyer, one on each side of the hall. Sheikh continues to walk with Montello into the living room, he sees two more bodyguards one on each side of the

Corinthian leather couch. In the middle of the couch sits Keon with a cup of tea already in hand. Taking a seat Montello gets comfortable in the Barcelona chair that's directly in Keon's view. Sheikh moves to the right of the chair standing quietly, while Keon continues to quietly sip the Earl Grey tea. Montello waits for acknowledgement, taking in the last sip of tea resulting in satisfaction, in a genuine tone, "That was so delicious, I didn't consider you having an eye for tea. I am quite surprised, I thought you to be more into abrasive drinks like Malt liquor. I have grown to enjoy Oolong tea, though it is a little early for me. It has a sweet refreshing citrus taste to it. You should enjoy some tea once in a while, a nice break from Hennessey or whatever you drink" he said. Keon enjoys letting people know their place, especially Montello, Montello being half human and half Fallen. On the flip-side Montello knew his desire for POWER is much stronger than his hatred for Keon, being a 'patsy' was part of the plan. He knows there will be a proper time to deal with Keon and The Sheol House, so he remains cool. The tension in the air is thin and yet is felt by everyone. The meeting proceeds "business as usual" as Montello continues on with the conversation.

"You have information about the delivery of the Crux of Baal from the Vatican." One of Keon's men hands a file in Montello's direction. Sheikh steps forward and takes the file. He begins to scan over it, while Keon explains, "Here are the routes, Passports and the name of my inside contact who can get you in the vault. You have resources including the information I just provided, so the rest is on you. I expect perfect execution as a return of my father's investment. You know that it is not necessary for me to explain the consequences of failure. I would hate for something like this to disrupt the lucrative flow of business." Without missing a beat Montello maintains his composure.

"Keon you worry way too much, I got this. You gotta have a little faith in me, I'm not going to fuck this up. This deal benefits you and me, for starters it will build a stronger trust between our Houses. Also, this is going to be a nice piece of change for my House. Most importantly you and your father, Lord Mephisto can overthrow the Dark Elders and rule Hades Realm. I don't plan to fuck shit up; my crew and I will be leaving for Italy next week. I am putting the finishing touches on the plan and waiting on info on how we are getting it out of the country. The equipment is in place already with my cousin overseeing everything till I arrive.

We're good so relax." Keon in fashionable sarcastic monotone "You are pretty smart Montello, for low-level management." Montello learned that dealing with Keon he had to be careful or it's your ass. He is very cruel and intelligent with no soul. He takes the condescending attitude from Keon, knowing that soon the Ajax Clan and the Sheol House will go to war with each other. So, for now he is buying time to prepare for when that day comes. The day will come when the Ajax Clan will no longer be the joke of the nation. This house will once again have the glory it once enjoyed. Montello remembers his father who was Fallen telling him that being half Fallen and human was going to put him in the line of fire. He was going to have to do whatever it takes to rule in this world. Keon is dressed in a 3-button white wool suit; humans would say this is not the color to wear in the middle of winter. He could care less for a human's limited imagination, his attitude towards them is that they are a waste of the universe. In his opinion what is the purpose of the universe having offspring? A being who is born not knowing who they are is a cruel and merciless fate. Keon thought why should he stoop to such a level as to consider human beings equal on any level. This is one of many reasons that he and his father, Mephisto Lynx turned their backs to the Dark Elders two years ago. Keon is carrying out his father's wishes to bring an end to the balance between Hades' Realm and Atum Celestial. Dark designs are in the works to usurp the Dark Elders' and the Nswts' influence and to rule both Hades Realm and Atum Celestial in the shadows. Keon considers himself to be the Face of Sheol House. On behalf of Lord Mephisto he has orchestrated alliances with several key members of the Dark High Council, those who answer to the Dark Elders. The leaders of these Houses follow his father's every command without hesitation and have a fear of the consequences. The Dark Elders have come to realize how powerless they are in addressing this betrayal. They are without proof and without full support of the remaining Houses of Hades Realm. The Law of Hades Realm is 'To rule with power or follow without question'. In turn Montello has declared a blood feud with Hannibal Guild. His motive is simple, his ambition is to gain power and influence for himself. Being a hybrid of Fallen and human (his mother who was African), he has no loyalty to either species. He rules the entire Westside of Chicago with an iron fist, from the suburb of Oak Park to Chicago's infamous East-West border of Roosevelt Road. He controls the Westside dope game, extortion, racket the whole underworld of the West side of Chi-town. Revenge is the fuel of Montello's ambition to be king and rule all of Chicago. To have his foot on the necks of those who look down upon him, especially Keon Lynx. Keon, a true High Fallen Elite, rules over the Near Northside of Chicago. White collar crime is his specialty along with inside trading. International arms deals and the global black market have kept them in power over Chicago's elite families Human and Fallen going on 100 years. Responsible for the murders and exploitation of members from the lower houses; anyone who opposes the will of the Dark Father. Keon cares less about the feud between the Hannibal Guild and the Ajax Clan, he just wants the order to be maintained. He looks down on Hannibal Guild because Cleopatra has the favor of the Dark Elders and he feels she is stepping out of her role. Truth be told she refused his advances and she have no interest in bonding with him or his House. She is cutting him off from the power and influence that Hannibal Guild has. Hannibal Guild stands as an obstacle to him and his father's plans to rule all. Keon sees Montello as a tool to bring Hannibal Guild to utmost desolation. When he was a young lord in court, he witnessed the drama between Hannibal Guild and Sheol House play out. Lord Mephisto and Lord Bacchus Rex debated issues and maneuvered the houses to power. However, Lord Rex was more methodical and therefore gained more influence. He also witnessed Cleopatra's ascension becoming Baroness after the assassination of her father. His contempt grew stronger as he watched her gain more support from the Dark Elders as a representative of the Hades Realm. Her role was crucial in orchestrating the delicate peace treaty between Hades Realm and Atum Celestial. Despite Keon being elevated to Viceroy of Sheol House, still he was not satisfied. Ego driven, to have power over Hannibal Guild to control Cleopatra. Now he's got someone to do the dirty work for him while remaining in the shadows untouched. He enjoys setting up the secret combinations to destroy those who may rise to power. He could care less about ruling Hades Realm and Atum Celestial, that's his Father's ambition. He just wants to put Cleopatra in her place. Keon and Montello have no love for each other; the goal they share is to destroy Hannibal Guild. Now "Your payment will be on time and in full, do I need to explain the cost of failure?" Keon's mind is in the now and present moment of business with Montello. Montello sighs to himself as he answers the comment, "Come on Keon, do you not think I overstand the levity of who you are and what you can do. I don't fail when it comes to my money, failure ain't my thing. Chill out man, if you are always going to tell me about failure, maybe you should think about not fucking with me at all."

Keon calmly replies, "I just want to make sure we have a healthy business relationship and things are going to plan. Excuse if I am a little cautious. We will meet in another two weeks."

They walk past Sheikh and as he approaches the elevator, Keon turns around for one final say. "I've heard that Michael Lee is coming for you, regarding those murders on the Belmont Rocks. Please allow me to send someone who will be your protection."

Montello smiles and addresses Keon in a proper forum, "I appreciate your help as always Lord Lynx but trust me I got this. I am expecting him to come, that's just how it is in the streets, I got eyes and ears all over." As the elevator doors open Keon enters along with his bodyguards "I look forward to the time Montello, when we BOTH have gained what we desire. You will enjoy the glory and the honor that is long overdue for your clan." Knowing in his heart, Keon is leaning towards Michael Lee decimating Montello. Using Montello's youth against him to cause chaos as a distraction from the real goal, of overthrowing Hannibal Guild along with Cleopatra. Montello is not fooled by the accolades and fake promises given by Keon. The resources provided by Keon and Sheol House he knows is a bunch of bullshit. He plays the game, the same game as Keon plays, the game for power.

CHAPTER 5

On the Southside Michael Lee is doing his weekly visit over his mother's house. Their relationship has come a long way since the kidnapping of Toni Ann. Michael Lee always felt that his mother blamed him for it. She did not approve of the lifestyle he was living, yet she knew it was necessary for his survival. Momma Leah blamed herself for not being able to give them a better life than they had when she was with Michael Lee and Toni Ann's father. It's been two years of intense discussions for Michael Lee and church for Momma Leah. "Come on Momma, I really do not want to go to the church social, someone is always asking when I'm coming to church. I can't even enjoy the food or the vibe without someone bringing me that 'Jesus stuff.' Ma you know how I feel about that topic. Jesus has his business and I have mine if he leaves mine alone, I won't tell him how to handle his. I respect your love because you are my Momma. No offense

Momma, to me religion is a hustle. A lot of folks are being played out of their money.

"Boy watch your mouth when you are talking about

a man of God. You say you respect me, listen to me when I say respect the Church and the Pastor. Besides, Serenity asked me about you." Michael Lee raises an eyebrow; he knew Serenity before he dropped out of high school. She convinced him to at least get his G.E.D., he has always seen her as a 'good girl'. Momma Leah notices the pause in the air around Michael Lee, she knew he liked Serenity, the only name of a girl who made him smile.

"Ma, can we not talk about church and all that. However, it would be good to see Serenity. I have been wondering how she is doing. Last time I saw her she was looking mighty nice in that blue dress. She always had a tight body, that booty is always bangin'."

Momma Leah smacks him on the shoulder, "You know better to talk to me like that boy, besides she's the Pastor's daughter. She ain't like those trifling ass little girls you mess with, look at you got me cussing and I heard a good message today." Michael Lee is laughing at his momma, Momma Leah is not one to take no mess when it comes to church, so she is trying not to laugh.

She smacks him again, "Don't play with the Lord boy, you know that I do not put up with that. You know in this house we respect the Lord and Jesus Christ; he has brought us a long way. And stop talking about Serenity's butt, you should not be looking at just that."

"I am sorry Momma my bad, I have some issues with that right now. I will respect that; you roll with Jesus.

I don't come around often, I want to just hang out with my family on Sunday dinner. You know how much I love your cooking, especially that fried chicken, baked macaroni, mustard greens, that sweet potato pie and all the good food a growing boy like me needs." Nobody can cook like my Momma; I place good money on that. I have been to a lot of places and heard a lot of folk talk about how their Soul food is. I'll always brag on my Momma's cooking, ain't nothing like it.

"Yo, where is Meekin? I have not seen her since I got here, she is usually your shadow."

Momma turns to Michael Lee, giving him that look when she believes and knows something is up. She motions him to come closer.

"I am whispering because I do not want Mimi to walk in while I am telling her business."

Michael Lee leans gets closer and smiles, "Momma you are always telling me her business."

Momma Leah smacks him again, "Hush boy, so what I can do that, I'm her granny. Anyway, Mimi met this boy and I don't like him. I am not too keen on any of her so-called friends. This boy, there's something about him, he plays this role like he is nice, but he ain't foolin' me."

Michael Lee rolls his eyes. "Ma you don't need to mess with Mimi's business and come to think of it you don't like anybody."

They both laugh out loud, "You can be a little too old fashion Ma, time isn't like when you grew up. If you want me to check him out, I can do that. She is my only niece and lately I have not been available for her."

Momma Leah pulls back with a worried tone in her voice. "I want to know what the scoop is, am I being too overbearing? You know how everybody says I am in their business," shaking her head as if the whole world doesn't overstand her. Since Toni Ann's disappearance, the memories of her smile, her laughter and both of them cooking together in the kitchen are more vivid. She has become more concerned and fearful when Mimi is not around at night. She is also concerned about Michael Lee, she always sees the hidden sadness behind his eyes. She knows he is blaming himself for not being there for them but the anger in the early days of Toni Ann's disappearance has mellowed. She has to be strong, so Michael Lee can forgive himself for the disappearance. For the whole family the first two years were a hard adjustment, it seems that everyone has come through but Michael Lee is taking a little longer. She likes to see him laugh and have a good time like when he was a little boy. He is better than he was since he has been hanging out with Sol, he is calmer. He is back to talking to her when he comes to his Sunday visits. She is worried about his work at Solid State Security. The broken bones, stitches across his face and bruises over his body are evidence of her concern. He's always gone but it seems that he doesn't mind the risk and the money is good. Hell, he has a job…just as long as the streets don't get him, I'm going to continue to thank the Lord Jesus. "Hurry up boy and set the table, the food is almost ready." Michael Lee once again is that little boy in her eyes.

As he washes his hands in the kitchen sink, he replies, "Bout time Momma, the food is calling my name, I'm starving."

CHAPTER 6

A few Brownstones down the block on 77th street, Michael Lee's best friends Ty and Cyril are hanging out in Ty's basement. The walls are adorned with pictures of Scarface and Big Booty Maxim models, being bathed by the sounds of Tupac in the background while playing PlayStation. Ty the more reasonable of the two calls out to Cyril who is struggling with the game.

"Pass the blunt man! You holding to the smoke too long. You sitting there bumping your gums about Tracy and loosing on Mortal Combat, nigga. You are not going to hit that she knows you are running game on her. You shouldn't have lied in the beginning."

Cyril's nonchalant vibe comes through his voice, "You worry too much cuz, I got this. Traci is just playing hard to get, when she decides to drop those panties, I am going to make it worth her wait. After tapping that ass so proper she'll be calling me 'doctor' Cyril and then I'll be making those house calls."

Ty blows out a long and very precise narrow line of smoke, responding sarcastically "This is some very good weed man, your imagination has been overactive, who you get it from? Really.... 'house calls' nigga... PLEASE! Ya know word on the street is that Traci is fucking that wack ass dude Byron. Your losing out to a wankster, so please don't fuck up my high." Cyril stops in the middle of the game.

"Just because I don't go to college nigga, stop lookin down on me, so what if all the ladies want to holla at you, doesn't mean you're better than me?"

Ty laughing, trying to hold in the smoke cuts back, "You on that shit again man, how long we've been boys? It was your dumb ass who left to go chase some girl to Minneapolis and she left you for another dude."

Cyril stands up, "I can't help it if the white girls there are built like Sistahs, fat asses and blondes can make a man want to try something new."

Ty passes the blunt back to Cyril, "Then learn to up your game as the 'Mack' you claim to be. Plus, I am sick of watching you get smashed in this lame ass video game. Turn to channel 7, I want to watch the 10 o'clock news and see some fucking current events."

Taking a deep pull off the blunt, Cyril blows a massive cloud in Ty's face. "I don't know who the fuck you think you are, but watch what you say to me. You know how I get down. You lucky you are my boy in other words I would fuck you up." Ty knowing Cyril's' routine when he gets faded, he always talks a lot of shit. They order a thin crust pepperoni from Tom's Pizza down the street, break bread then Cyril falls asleep.

The Anchorman speaking in his T.V. voice, "Thank you Marie for the weather report, a lot of folks will be getting up early to warm up their cars and clear their driveways. Summing it up in one-word...COLD. Now tonight's top story.... Chicago's Near Northside in the grip of gruesome murders at the Belmont Rocks. We have Channel 7 News very own Ace Bosworth here to report the latest developments."

"The increased presence of Chicago P.D. intensifies the fear that has already gripped the community of Chicago's Lakefront area. Residents feel they are no longer safe. Officers have gone as far as to interrupt lovers sitting on the park benches after 6 p.m. and street performers are no longer present. No weekend barbecues or visitors walking along the lakeside enjoying the view of Lake Michigan at night. In this ongoing investigation police have no leads... no arrests. People are demanding answers. Anybody could be the perpetrator and anyone can be a victim." The news report fades into the background being old news to Ty and Cyril. Ty nudges Cyril, "Hey man you slipping, pass the blunt.

I bet they are looking for someone black, you know how these Pigs are. They ain't nowhere to be found when REAL shit is happening. Where were they when motherfuckas were getting murc'd?"

Cyril stands and begins grind dancing in place. "Fuck tha police man, I am trying to get faded for this party later on tonight. I am looking to get my groove on and getting in Traci's panties tonight, fuck that mark ass Byron. He ain't gon' do shit but stand there and watch."

Catching the look on Cyril's face, Ty laughs, "I saw Sonia Monday at Tom's Pizza with that big ass, the way she's looking I'm aiming for gold, I am going to hit that, watch me." Cyril stops in the middle of his dance with indignation across his face.

"What's happening at the Belmont Rocks is bullshit. I go there sometimes to be alone and think when I got some real shit on my mind. I got this feeling that these cats are familiar with us. The scene feels like we are being watched or some shit, it's like they are waiting for us. That's why I trust Mike when he says he knows what's up, demons, zombies and other, crazy ass shit that we have seen hanging with that dude. Shit you see in movies and comic books, the same shit that nightmares are made of." Ty snatches the blunt out Cyril's unaware grip, taking a long toke. Closing his eyes while enjoying the smoke, as it travels through his body straight to the dome. Opening his eyes, he continues to talk to Cyril's half assed attention.

"For me to get thru this shit I need to relax man. Next Friday we're gonna handle that shit like business as usual. Michael Lee needs everyone on deck, especially us. Feel me on that man, real talk."

Ty slaps Cyril's head to drive the point home, the sensation brings Cyril to his natural self. "Nigga I heard you, what the fuck you hitting me for? Yo' I'll fuck you up if you do that shit again."

Ty smiles in response "You ain't gonna do shit, here take this back with your brain-dead ass."

Cyril smiles as he retrieves the prized blunt, "Yea Dawg, we got this, you act like I haven't been in this dance before. I got Mike's back more than you do, all this fear talk is fucking my high up. Let's go to Cookie's for some medicine then bounce over to this party on 95th in Jeffery Manor. Sonia said she would be coming with a friend, so you need to keep her friend occupied while I holla at Sonia."

Ty shakes his head…"Man, the things you do so you can get some ass. So, I'm looking at a bag of 20 White Castles, large fries and a strawberry shake. Short me even ONE White Castle, next time you're on your own. Remember that wack ass party 2 weeks ago? The chick you left me with, all she talked about was how her last dude fucked her over. It was a good thing I was faded listening to her, that conversation would have driven a saint to drink. By the way, you still owe me for that one so adds some onion rings."

Cyril passes the blunt to Ty, "How many times you gonna bring that up, my bad. Shit, I didn't get any that night."

Ty snaps back, "Ya think, you keep forgetting that one very important thing."

Cyril looks at him with one eyebrow raised, "What the fuck is that?"

Ty smiling with ALL 32 teeth pauses, "Brotha you gots no game when it comes to women. You can whoop on a gang of dudes but you can't get one female to drop the panties."

Cyril slapping the middle of his chest with the blunt in his mouth. "The fuck you say!?... I got plenty game; I gets ass ALL the time."

Ty gets up, draws back the curtain, looking into the night as the new snow falls. "I'm getting tired of just sitting here. Let's go see how good the Sistahs are looking tonight, maybe there is a Queen for me. I doubt it though, I like a natural Sistah, dark skinned, locs, thick ass and a hell of a mind. You don't find that many where we are heading." Cyril pulls in another deep toke and blows out again. "Seriously man… that's your problem, you have high standards when it comes to a woman. Believe me or not bruh, I like to meet a Sistah like that. You gotta make do with what we have around here."

Ty looking away from the window asks his friend, "So... you are saying I should just settle? That is some shit I ain't gonna do, way too many crazy ass chicks around here. Damn cuz I know you high, but I aint that high to start listening to some dumb shit like that. Now get your coat so we can leave, you've been crying about this party all night long."

Cyril finishes the last of the blunt. "Hey man I gotta take a piss I'll meet you outside, go get the car started."

Ty grabs his P-Coat out of the closet, "Now you want me to warm the car for you? I'm not your fucking maid dude."

Cyril shouts down the hall, "Just start the car man, I am taking a piss."

As Ty shouts out the apartment door, "Hurry the hell up then!" Walking outside to the car Ty pulls out his keys to the '69 Red Chevy Malibu, the cleanest car on the block. Looking up at the night sky, he sees the stars and feels the crisp cold air cascading over his face. "Man... Its fucking cold out here, too cold to even look at the stars."

DIRTY SAINTS

He sees the Big Dipper, the Little Dipper and begins to stare at Orion's Belt, the three stars are in a perfect alignment. He begins to wonder to himself, "Amazing, if there is a god, he does some real shit."

CHAPTER 7

"Yo, Ty" ... an unfamiliar voice calls him by name. He turns to see a tall and dark figure dressed in all black. Standing there Ty begins to feel an intimidating and dangerous aura, this person resonates with an ominous purpose.

Ty asks, "Do I know you?" No answer.

"I am speaking to you bruh this silent treatment doesn't work with me. Trying to scare me and shit is not going to help you." Walking towards the stone silent figure, Ty reaches inside his coat. With his left-hand toward the right breast of his jacket to pull out the waiting Glock. Ty asking again steps away from his car, distancing himself into the street.

"I'm gonna ask again, do I know you?" The figure still silent, pulls the wool cap right above his eyes.

"Nigga... I'm asking for the last time; do I know you?" Responding in a sinister and deep voice.

"No, you don't know me, but WE do know you. We know Cyril, we know Sol, and we definitely know Michael Lee. We know that you are taking on the Ajax Clan."

Ty moves the safety off the Glock, "I don't know what the fuck you're talking about, I don't know anybody you just mentioned. Now if you don't step off, there could be a problem. I am sure you or whoever the fuck, has mistaken me for someone else." The figure continues ignoring the warnings given by Ty.

"We are not mistaken; you humans have a distinct odor; it's how predators hunt. Once a hunter has that distinct scent there is no mistake and the hunt are on." Instincts quickly take over and Ty begins firing into the side of the brown brick building. Missing, Ty runs into the park across the street. He played in this park as a boy, he knows that there's not many trees for cover. He decides to use the playground equipment as an obstruction from a clear shot; from anyone aiming at him. He runs then slides behind a pink castle he used to hide from bullies back in the day. A flash of wind passes by calling out to him.

"You are going to die tonight and then your friend when he comes to find you." Another flash of wind closer to his ear, "Then we are going to begin to kill all of your family, your Momma who lives on 83rd and Exchange on the East side, near that Pepe's Taco you like to eat." Another flash of wind, a high-speed shadow moving from spot to spot. "We know all about you and your friends, there is nothing you can do. I am here to take your life, the lives of your homies, the lives of everyone you even though you loved or hated. Even the women you have fucked in the past." Then there is laughter "Look at you, can't even shoot, you can't even see where to fire your gun, humans are so fragile. Your species is SOOO pathetic, easy to manipulate and so easy to murder. You have no intelligence knowing when to quit, you are beaten."

Ty buying time is waiting for Cyril, hoping he heard him popping off the shots. The voice in the night continues to call him out, Ty knowing if he moves, it's over. Ty's panicked conscious is working to remain calm; fighting his natural instinct to get up and fire. The Shadow's laughter becomes more insidious and maniacal, ringing in his ears. Poking at all his weaknesses with an unsettling vibration, lack of courage.

Thoughts running rampant in his mind, "Come on nigga, body this motherfucka! Ain't nobody fuckin' with my fam, especially my mom's! Shit I don't want that to happen! I gotta protect everyone I love! I just can't sit here and wait to die! What the fuck, I got to end this now!"

The overpowering urge to give up, his immobilizing anger, a sense of loss and feeling of absolute failure consumes his thoughts. His emotions are desynchronizing his cool disposition, he is lost in this moment.

"Where the fuck is Cyril's dumb ass?" Suffering this cerebral chaos and lost in deep thought. In the midst of all this mental anarchy swells a quiet and evil whisper which pierces through the numbness of his psyche. The Shadow speaks to Ty with a calm psychotic tone.

The one scent I love the most about the odor of humans is complete acceptance of powerless subjugation to the inevitability of death. Every human that I have slaughtered reeks of it, the satisfaction that I get is so intoxicating."

Instantaneously the Shadow has one hand around Ty's neck strangling him. He begins gasping for air seeing the darkness of the faceless shadow with red pupils appearing in a black backdrop. A sinister smile appears containing an elation of absolute joy from conquest.

"You see human, I like the buildup too, the sight of dripping and profuse sweat. The result from the emotional torture that I perform so rigorously. I enjoy the anticipation of the kill and how much of a thrill I get. I have you by your throat watching hope you fight for your useless life. I am ready to bust a nut, the thought of my cum burning any of a life you thought you had, as your soft flesh glistens."

He begins squeezing harder, he starts punching Ty in the stomach, each punch harder than the last. Each punch aligned with laughter, embracing demonic pleasure of causing torment. Ty's body slowly goes limp, blood dripping from his mouth, his head lays aside with the appearance of a broken neck. Seeing the results of his work the demon automatically loosens his grip; the sensation of victory has taken full effect. After looking over Ty's seemingly lifeless body he finally releases his death grip. Ty falls knees first, his body slumps over and his face falls hitting the ground. Looking down at Ty, the Shadow stands salivating after having his demonic appetite filled and satisfied.

With a shallow voice Ty slowly begins to speak. "Yo ass wipe you seem to have gotten ahead of yourself. Don't assume we didn't… we didn't know you were following us. You are so busy thinking that me and my boy are just a couple knuckleheads… who… just smoke weed and look at women." The Shadow pulls back, the thought creeps off his lips,

"You should be dead, I just thoroughly fucked your ass up. I am surprised that you are still able to talk, I just beat the shit out of you."

Ty laughs despite being bruised. "Surprise !!!" Ty looks up at the Shadow forcing a smile, "You are not getting out of this bruh, my crew also knows WHO and WHAT you are. NO WAY you are getting out of this dick head. We are going to completely fuck up the Ajax Clan and Montello's bitch ass, as a matter of fact you are not going to be around." Ty is now being lifted off the ground choke hold style, the demon fully pissed off.

"Guess what motherfucka, I am gonna snatch your heart out and devour it, that's the last thing you are going to see human!"

Coughing up blood, Ty trying not to laugh. "Wait... wait... wait... before you eat my heart, hold up one second There's something I gotta tell you before I body your ass, can I say my last words in peace?" The Shadow pauses, then he slowly pulls Ty closer.

Ty struggles to whisper, "You should really look behind you." The Shadow pauses and grins, "FUCK YOU the Shadow screams, I am not falling for that shit."

Ty gathers strength and continues to offer the warning, "You should really turn around." The Shadow continues to threaten. "It's time to end yo' ass." Drawing back his free hand for the killing blow, the Shadow suddenly feels a presence on the scene. The question comes to the Shadow's mind, "Where is this feeling coming from?" NOW.... His inner voice becomes louder, more urgently saying to him, "TURN AROUND!!!".

Ty's voice has gotten stronger and more confident, "Now you were saying that shit about killing my fam, my enemies and even the women I used to fuck? You really fucked up and I mean fucked up in a major way, by threatening to kill my moms and my sister. For the record motherfucka, I bodied a lot of your homies and I am going to continue to ice even more, starting with you fool." As soon as the Shadow turns, he meets a jaw crushing blow that comes with the clarity that the tables have turned. Cyril unleashed an unforgiving blow to the Shadows jaw, that sinks him to the ground like a sack of potatoes. Looking up immediately the Shadow meets a 12-gauge pump action shotgun pointed in his face.

"My dude, I didn't hear shit. I was on the phone with one of the homies, who's already at the party telling me some shit about Sonia coming with some dude. I was venting and shit, trying to take a one-handed piss. I came out of the bathroom and looked out the window, and didn't see you. Right off the muscle I felt some bullshit was going down. I went to the closet, grabbed my Big Baby, bounced out the door and ran into the park. Where I saw this mark ass, piece of shit, getting ready to ice your ass. Nigga how many times have I told to do a 360 view of your environment? I had to handle listening to this piece of shit running his fucking mouth about how he was going to kill us and shit. It was VERY hard to listen to this clown ass motherfucka talking and really pissing me off watching him whoop on yo' ass. I was just waiting for the moment to get the drop on this bitch ass demon and body this motherfucka."

Ty staggers towards Cyril, standing with all his will in place, looking down at the bleeding Shadow.

"Ya know I find humor in what you are saying and at the same time embarrassed like a motherfucka, knowing that you were watching me getting my ass whooped." Ty starts laughing despite grimacing in pain.

"As usual you came thru when I was in a tight spot, thanks man, I love you bruh" Cyril holding his aim reestablishing his grip on the shotgun at the Shadow, he smiles.

"What now, do what it do to those cats who threaten us and our loved ones? Ty, ya know I am feeling a certain way right about now bruh?" Cyril looks at Ty, fatal eyes meet fatal eyes. The evening wind offers a song of peaceful meditation and as the song ends the sound of a shotgun and Glock bellows the last note. Leaving a portrait of an abstract painting, red stain in the snow followed by footprints, as Ty and Cyril walk out of the park.

Cyril non-chantly asks, "How about going to get some pizza?"

CHAPTER 8

In Chicago's Gold Coast Streeterville area, Cleopatra awaits the arrival of a towel in her lavish bathroom of the innermost part of the exclusive penthouse. Sitting in her jasmine and milk morning bath, a maid hurriedly comes in with a very large and plush towel. Cleopatra arises as she grabs the towel, exiting the tub. Looking at herself in the full-length mirror, smiling and complimenting the reflection of beauty as she dries herself. In her mind-speak her day begins as it always does with an affirmation.

"Girl today and forever is your day; speak as an angel and play while being the devil."

She continues to smile at herself humming, the maid stands waiting for the next command. The peace is soon interrupted,

"Baroness! Baroness! apologies for interrupting your bath. My Grace, we have news of the murders and it's of utmost importance and cannot wait." The switch from Cleo to Baroness was an instant.

"I shall allow you this interruption this ONE and only time Lord Obi. Even if you are my brother it would be foolish to do it again, now speak." Lord Obi Rex, the youngest brother of Cleopatra Rex, is captain of her personal guard and advisor.

"My Baroness, our sources report just as you knew what would happen, Keon Lynx and Montello Roy have met for the final details of retrieving the Crux of Baal. They are moving tomorrow night and Montello's operatives are in place at The Vatican. They are waiting for Montello's arrival the next morning and later that evening they are going to make their move." Cleo walks to her bedroom as Obi follows, she remains silent, listening very intently to what is being said.

Obi continues, "Our plant on the inside is getting more nervous, he feels he will be found out at any moment and he requests to be withdrawn immediately." Cleopatra glides through the French doors that lead to her master bedroom with its California King size bed and lavish Egyptian décor. Two servants with clothing and accessories are waiting. She allows the towel to fall to the carpeted floor, she stands on a very plush red carpet, designed with ancient symbols and the Crest representing Hannibal Guild.

"I want a car ready and dinner reservations at The Clue for 10 pm. They better not give my favorite table to anyone. Let's just buy out the restaurant for the night and double what they ask for. I want eyes on Michael Lee at all times and do not intervene. If anyone from our guild has an issue with Michael Lee, they'll answer me with their death. Michael Lee is after our brother and I am after the reason our brother has disappeared. There is a bigger plan with bigger fools leading the way, I am going to stop this from affecting the whole of Hades Realm. I want to see the lowlifes who wish to bring chaos to this house. Michael Lee is very capable of handling anything, anyone and everything."

She murmurs, "I like that about him, a human like him is rare. I just want to see for myself who exactly our enemies are." Keon will pay for his indiscretions, exercising after all his own will without my permission. I know that Keon and Mephisto are making moves to usurp the Dark Elders. I promise myself they will BOTH lick my boots, to my COMPLETE
satisfaction."

Obi turns to exit, "I will handle this matter personally."

Before he exits Cleopatra softly speaks to her brother, "I want you to be extra careful, I do not trust our uncle. Watch your conversations around him. I have information that he has been consorting with Keon on several occasions. After the council meetings and parties that we have attended, has he been wanting to talk to you alone?" Obi pauses, he thinks of past events and conversations that his uncle has approached him about. The conversations about Michael Lee and his sisters' relationship and operations of The Network. He begins connecting the dots, which brings to light of what his sister is speaking on.

"It would be disheartening for our uncle to be a traitor and usurper. He would be stripped of ALL including the family name, we will have to turn him over to The Network so they can punish him."

There is a sadness in his heart over this, Obi at one time was very close to his uncle and wanted to be like him. His father Bacchus didn't pay him or Apas as much attention as he did to Cleopatra. Obi knew he was not as ruthless as his sister, nor was he rebellious like Apas. Cleopatra saw a level of loyalty in Obi that's a valuable asset which aids her to rule Hannibal Guild. In turn, she guided her brother to the position that he holds today. There had been talk of nepotism because of him being the Baroness brother. Obi's ability to see and predict the moves of the enemies of Hannibal Guild was unmatched on the battlefield. His involvement with The Network in using the intel they gathered brought about the truce between Hades Realm and Celestial Atum. Cleopatra continues, "I want every detail, as your Baroness I order you to spy on Lord Bilal Rex. As your sister I am asking you to protect the family's name." Obi looks at his sister, "I do this for Hannibal Guild and the name of Rex, our family's legacy." Cleopatra sits down in the chair; without a word several racks of high-end clothing are brought in and jewelry is presented. Gazing over the diamond rings, gold chains and other trinkets she contemplates. She knows that her uncle is guilty and how this will affect Obi.

She feels his kindness is out of place in the game of power, yet a useful tool to get close to their uncle. Sister, I have not forgotten, I am of the House of Rex and my duties as director of the Network, I serve with due diligence. It is my responsibility to neutralize all enemies and opposition." Cleopatra smiles as Obi exits, she knows that her brother and The Network are going to do what it takes.

"Tonight's dinner is going to get interesting; I wonder what Michael Lee likes to eat.?" The question of what to wear is at the forefront, "I think this would be a good start" as she pulls from the rack, a simple red bow knot Peplum Design coat and pants set, accessorized with a pair of Christians Louboutin black with red-sole ankle boots. "What will Michael Lee like?" she ponders.

CHAPTER 9

Rolo slowly opens his eyes, to see that his arms and hands are not tied. Getting up very slowly off the cot in a room with a single light bulb hanging from the ceiling. On the table he sees food and something to drink, a chair to sit down on. As he walks, he stumbles regaining his facilities. Sitting down in the chair he picks up the sandwich, begins inspecting it for any unusual smell and contents. He picks up the glass to the smell of apple juice and slowly drinks. As he takes his final bite, the door opens. A tall muscular dark-skinned woman walks in the room. She's in good shape, medium height and short locs on a half-shaved head adds to her attractiveness.

"I am very glad to see that you enjoyed your meal, we didn't want you to go hungry and get thirsty." Rolo takes his time as he chews the last piece of the sandwich. He stares up at the woman standing in front of him and calmly asks, "Who the fuck is you and where the fuck am I?" Smiling she politely replies in the most tender of tones as she sits down.

"Good, I see that you don't need any medical attention, you are aware and alert. To answer your first question, the answer is simple; I am here to make sure you are taken care of. I am also here to make sure you stay put. Those are the only questions I am going to answer." Rolo looks around as Shammi talks, he sees no windows, only a toilet in the corner and a single roll of toilet paper on the floor.

"Sistah… I don't know what this is all about but one way or another I'm gettin' out of here. So how about we cut the dumb shit and just take me to your fuckin leader."

Shammi smiles, "Look at you, all manly... ready to get at me. Like I said, I am here to make sure you are well taken care of. My leader, my king wants to chat with you. As a matter of fact, he should be coming thru that door any second now." Rolo's attention is drawn away from Shammi, as the door creaks while slowly opening. Sol calmly enters the room, giving Shammi a hug and a kiss.

"Baby you know how much I love your hugs and kisses. They give me that strong feeling of being human." Hitting Shammi's' voluptuous ass, she smiles and walks to the side of the table. Rolo seeing this affection, disrupts with a loud sigh. Sol sits down across from him.

"I thought we should sit and talk; you know to avoid any unpleasantness. You my friend are the solution to avoid people from dying. I personally am not one for violence, in my own opinion it's never a first choice." Hoping his calm demeanor will ease Rolo's' defiant attitude to a degree of logic. Yet looking across the table he knows this is NOT the case.

"I am not saying a mothafuckin' thing, so do your worse. You trying this calm shit on me... come on man, I see the bullshit right off the bat."

Rolo leans back in the chair and folds his arms. Sol continues, "To conclude my thoughts about violence allow me to share a statement of Brother Malcolm, 'I only condone violence as a means of SELF DEFENSE' "I am trying to help you, so let me ask you this, are you part of the Ajax Clan?"

Rolo smiles unfolding his arms, leans in close to Sol. Rolo takes a moment, realizes that he can be himself, "You know already what set I belong to. Yea, I belong to the Ajax Clan and that is ALL you dumb asses are gonna get from me. So, save your breath, I ain't talking."

Sol maintains the line of questioning, continuing with the steady and slow deliverance. "So, are you involved in the recent murders? Could you give me the reason? Who is Montello Roy working for and what's the plan?"

Highly annoyed again Rolo leans back in the chair, "Like I said... I am not telling you shit!" Sol smiles, "I see you're big on loyalty, that's a good thing. Protecting your homies, to stay true to the cause and maintaining the circle. I admire that in anyone, friend and foe. I am trying to save you a lot of 'unnecessary' pain. Can I tell you a story? I am sure you don't mind; we have plenty of time. Back home it was always peaceful, a peace that human minds can't imagine. Their idea of heaven is not even close to describing my home. Now I am here on earth in this dimension. I overstand having that young and exciting body has given you the chance to fully experience humanity. The first thing I know is that humans, well they can be a handful. Working with Michael Lee has given me that experience. Three years for me is not enough time to get fully comfortable while in this space, though I have managed quite well. I feel every day that I am with him I have to commit my whole self to him. I see him hurt each and every time he kills an opponent in battle. It is quite brutal and I have no taste for that. I am just a humble Ntru, a rookie in eternity terms. I got a few more decades to go, here I go talking about me.... sorry."

"Man... I don't give a damn about you or Michael Lee, his momma and his family, I don't give a fuck about humans. If you ask me sounds like you two are butt-fucking. I have an idea; you can just let me go and my crew and I will just get you and this BITCH... maybe I will give this Michael Lees' family a pass. Because all I can remember is being with this chick at this party at the Cat House. I was having a VERY good time drinking and blowing trees. The only annoying thing was, that this dude trying to get at the chick I was with. He kept trying to be slick and shit, then finally his boy got him out of my face. All I know is I was about to get some ass we were walking to her car and then I woke up here. So, you can pretend to be nice all day, and I am still not going to say a fucking thing."

Sol leans in with sincere kindness, "I am going to give you a piece of advice. It seems you must have always wanted to come to earth, many of us have that desire. Once I was immature, not listening to wise counsel of the Elders. I crossed boundaries that I was not supposed to cross. The result was encountering a more powerful and older being who had more resolve and maturity. He was definitely going to kill me without question. As I was about to die the second death, I was then saved by a human. He just did what he felt he needed to do, not thinking it was right or wrong. Michael Lee saved my life force, he often says that ALL of us Ntru and otherworld beings are full of shit and hypocritical. Fighting the dark tendencies within himself, some days are better than others, yet he stays on his path to do what is right. That is why I ... have his back to the very end. I will always support him wanting to be in charge of his own destiny. You agreed to give up something in return for this experience on earth. I bet you accepted their or his offer knowing what it would cost you. They picked this body of this young man who was on the verge of giving up on life.

This young man who was calling out in desperation and anger, finally he received an answer. We both know how temptation works, wanting something so bad you do anything to get it. All that anger and desperation was interpreted as chaos orders. Ask yourself, is this worth the second death, dying while being someone else's bitch? Is this worth Michael Lee killing you?"

Rolo stands up calmly from the chair, "You have no idea who you are fucking with cuz, you should have restrained me. You know who I am, but you have no idea of what I am capable of!!" He begins to transform to his Fallen form. Sol sits quietly observing the transformation as he continues with his story.

"As I was saying, friend, I still have a lot to learn about human beings. I do know this, that some humans desire peace not for just themselves, but for their family and others. They go to church, help their elders, they try to do the right thing. Then you have the humans who choose to be weak, hateful and they want to destroy innocence. Disrupting calm, they don't care, allowing their inner demons to rule. They've given up on all that is good on earth."

Rolo retorts in a feral voice, "I am not saying nothing, so keep your philosophical views and shove them up your ass. I don't give a fuck about this human nature thing you are speaking of. You are going to let me out of this room or I am going to kill both of you. Talk to someone who fucking cares, because I don't. I am not just here just to have the human experience."

Sol asks again, "Then why are you here?" Rolo smiles, "Are you deaf, I ain't saying shit. I will be returning to

Hades Realm as a powerful and influential Lord and Celestial Atum, time is coming to an end. There is nothing you and your crew can do to stop it."

Sol sighs, knowing he is not getting through, "Point taken friend, as you have said you don't care about anything. It is very unfortunate; you had your chance to do the right thing by telling us what's happening."

Rolo laughing out loud, "BIIIIIIITCH PLEASE, what the fuck are going to do if I don't sing!? A bunch of ghetto ass clowns saving the world. Get the fuck outta here with that bull shit!"

Rolo laughs even louder, "I know after my crew finds out it was you who snatched me up, all y'all are through!"

In an instant Rolo's head is slammed through the wooden table. Standing over him in a chastising tone, "My king was offering you a way out, and you shouldn't be rude by calling him a bitch. Not cool, now you are going to learn shit the hard way." Shammi without much effort picks Rolo up and throws him against the wall. Sol wanted to step in but pauses remembering the agreement they made when it came to situations like these. She would allow him to talk before physical force is needed. Rolo asked for this, so he doesn't feel any guilt while Shammi does her thing. Her model looks resembling that of an ebony amazon, 5'11 with a solid 160 and a well-muscled frame reflecting flexible organic steel. She is a conduit of power and beauty; she can crush an ego with a single body slam. Back in her party girl days she ran with entertainers and athletes alike. That all ended one night at a house party in the affluent neighborhood of Pill Hill, Chicago's premiere black neighborhood on South Paxton Ave. was where she was raped 5 years ago. Two years of therapy cleared her mind, at times revisiting the memories were painful and she wanted to quit. Once she got going the next move was to strengthen her body. She started training in boxing, Jiu- jitsu and Aikido. She met Sol when Michael Lee saved her friend Pamela from a Fallen. Before that she never heard of the Fallen, she went to confront the being who assaulted her friend. For a good while she was holding her own, the boxing and Jiu-Jitsu was paying off. As she had him in an armbar, all of sudden he transformed to his true image. Sliding out of the armbar he began to beat her with the intent of killing her. When he was about to finish her off Sol came crashing through the living room window. At that same moment Michael Lee decapitated the still smiling Fallen. That was the first time that she met Sol, after that they would hang out sometimes, she would see Michael Lee at times but he always kept his distance. Seeing Sol as some sort of angel, though she never believed in shit like that. The more she heard the rumors of demons and all types of action on the Southside her curiosity grew even more. The more the streets talked about this dude and his crew taking them out, the closer she wanted to be to them. One night she followed them to an abandoned house on the West Side near Pulaski, where children's remains were being found. As she watched Michael Lee fight the more, she wanted to be involved. She was a witness to the reasons why Michael Lee fights and who he is. He was fighting not just to kill a murderer but in his own way to protect innocence. She also saw the value of Sol and Michael Lee's friendship; they were family. This was the moment she realized the value of Sol to her; she knows who he really is. At first, they didn't want her involved, but she knew a lot of ballers and her beauty got her in every club on the Near North Side. Sol wanted her to stay away from the work due to the deep feelings he has for her.

Two years last month and still working out the kinks.

"Damn baby you knocked him out cold, we have to be careful with this one." Poking the unconscious Rolo to see if there are any signs of life, she picks him up and lays him on the cot. Brushing her locks away from her face, "Baby you know how I feel about people calling you out of your name, I just snap sometimes."

Sol contemplates his next move, "I need more info on the relic, we need to know Montello's full involvement with Keon."

Sol gets up from the table and walks towards Shammi. "Baby I am hungry, that how about you? I am in the mood for some fish, let's go grab some at Josie's Joint. I heard it's really good, have you been yet?"

Shammi jumps with unexpected delight. "You must have felt my energy, I have worked up an appetite dealing with this moron. He was really pushing it, I was ready to go off on this dumb ass. He is lucky I just knocked his punk ass out."

Sol smacks her on her heart shaped muscled ass, as she slowly walks in front of him, "Baby I am so glad you overstand me, that is one of the things I dig about you." As she turns the corner outside the basement door, "I know."

Hours later the room remains quiet, the energy of Shammi and Sol has left the room. Rolo begins to come back to life, first with a twitch of his finger, then the sudden jump into panicked animation, "THAT BITCH!!" He pauses looking around the empty room, rubbing his head. "When I see that chick again, the things I'm gonna do to her before I kill her."

He stands, looking off in the distance, for a long minute he gathers his bearings. Walking towards the door angry and without thinking, he kicks it open. "Fuck this if that bitch is waiting on me, I got something for that ass." He steps through the door into unexpected freedom looking to the left he sees a T.V. Looking right he sees the backdoor, holding his breath he edges to the door. As he reaches it, he checks to see if it's locked and finds the deadbolt easy to turn without sound. Once out the door he runs full speed down the alley, not concerned and with great joy he shouts …"I am the fuck outta here!"
START HERE

CHAPTER 10

Night time is the life time, when everything is 'poppin'. The Sphere is the hottest spot for House music on Chicago's North Side. The dance floor is packed synchronizing to the sounds of Frankie Knuckles. It's Friday night and the energy pulsates like the rhythm of a heartbeat. Amongst those who dance are those who make sure the heart beat continues. Lowkey security prepares for a quiet meeting of two, instructions over the com link.

"Team 7... Michael Lee will be in your sights in 20 seconds, let him through. Be advised that Commander Rex has arrived on sight." The Network, an organization with the skill to get any and all intelligence, with paramilitary skills above any human intelligence agencies.

Obi's commanding voice comes over the line, "This is Commander Rex, we are in Status Alpha. All team leaders this is a 'need to know, any issues address them to myself immediately. Initiate protocols for areas C, D, and H to Hades level 6 and maintain your positions." All teams reply, "Yes, my Lord."

SOBEK KHASKHEMWY MERI RA

All eyes are on Michael Lee as he descends down the red and black steps, he enters the restaurant. The Clue is a quiet space for conversations and other designs to be unseen and unheard. Cleo, enjoying a glass of Shiraz, examines the color and smells the bouquet of flowers on the table. "I see you have outdone yourself Antwon, your taste in wine is impeccable. You have never let me down, that is why I love coming here... I feel so 'royal'. Antwon is a tall, dark skinned and lean man who stands more than six feet tall. Immigrated from Cape Town, South Africa, having an accent that flows; projecting an elegant aura. He takes his service to Cleo very seriously, making sure HER EVERY REQUEST is met by any means.

"Will your guest be arriving soon, we are preparing lamb, a very delicate meat; don't want it to dry Baroness." After taking a sip, Cleo savors the flavor of the red and deeply rich wine. "Yes, Antwon he will be on time. Who would miss having dinner with me?"

"I am beginning to feel a little underdressed." Hearing his voice Cleo smiles, taking another sip of wine. "So, this is your idea of dinner, you are aware this is a discussion about the murders on the Belmont Rocks? Remember, we will be talking about those assholes, Montello and Keon... doesn't that kill your appetite?" Cleopatra ignores Michael Lee's satire, she smiles

"Antwon here was just a little concerned about your arrival." Antwon is caught off guard by Michael Lee's sudden appearance and quickly regains his composure.

"I will check on the lamb Mistress." Abruptly excusing himself, he brushes past paying no attention to Michael Lee at all. Michael Lee smiling as he sits, "I don't think he likes me much. I can't stay long, I gotta meet my boy Sol over in Evergreen Park. Cleo sighs, "You and the Southside." Taking off his black wool full length coat and black gloves.

"That's home ya feel me? It's where I go to get away from all this bullshit over here with you and these crazy ass white folks." They pause in each other's eyes, a short tense moment of two very powerful energies. Then Cleopatra smiles, she can't but respect him. "Lately I've got this feeling, this is the 'calm before the storm', before all hell breaks loose."

She pulls the deep red cloth napkin and lets it fall covering her lap. "I thought we would enjoy some food and conversation, as you would say 'break bread'." Michael Lee had to admit he liked that Cleopatra had a little bit of hood lingo. For Michael Lee TRUST comes with time and effort. Due to recent events, he sees that a much bigger picture has begun to unfold. For this reason, he has agreed to this alliance, in the beginning Michael Lee argued with himself to ask Cleopatra for help. Once again reason set in, he had to be smart. He sent a message by snitch to Hannibal Guild, the response he received said that Cleopatra found his sister alive. And now that Ty and Cyril have been attacked by a group of assassins called the Shadow this raises the stakes even higher. The beginning of this alliance was uneasy, he still feels that Fallen are a plague to existence; they are only to be destroyed. Thinking of his family, they truly don't have any idea of what is going on in his life. His aunts were always telling his mother that he was spoiled and protected. They were not even involved when shit was deep which was fine with him. He will protect them regardless of their opinions of him. His mother always says that his family does love him but he ain't buying it. He remembers how they treated him differently from his other cousins. Their children are the "crown jewels" of the family. He's the "black sheep" the family fuck-up, as a matter of fact he now enjoys being the "rebel." He smiles coming back to the world, leaving his thoughts for a later time.

STEELING his thoughts on the task at hand, he realizes that this dinner has put him on a much higher level. It's not just to kill every Fallen only, it's deciding which humans as well. This alliance is the pin that has burst his bubble of prejudice against Fallen. Back on the block he just wanted to be the next ghetto superstar. He was cool doing his hustle, blowing trees and hitting the finest ass he could get his hands on. He was living his life, not this battle for the souls of man. Now he sees the real picture, even though he doesn't overstand everything that's going on. Seeing beings like Sol and Cleopatra, he has also fought Arc-Fiends. He has encountered the Marked Ones, the humans who have aligned themselves with the Arc-Fiends. Now he has met friends, other 'Black Sheep" who have his back. He was once in a situation of being outnumbered, where he was aided by the homeless. These common people yielded their power to him, where he overcame the enemy therefore saving his life. Because of this event his intentions and thoughts have shifted, he is just not fighting for himself or his sister. Now this third year of this new life he is seasoned and has grown accustomed to all that has happened. Nothing phases him, he knows that he has just entered… WAR.

"I remember sneaking in here, when it was the Playground. I miss the golden age of House music. CATS, like Farley Keith in my opinion, is the Father of Chicago House music. Kenny "Jamin" Jason, the only white boy who knew real House and finally Bad Boy Bill. In those days this place was packed... balls to walls, now that I see it today; I didn't know a restaurant could fit. The music is still banging and the crowd is stuck up as ever… "It fits you Sistah." Being in an unfamiliar place he turns in every direction of the restaurant, not liking having his back to the door, a habit he developed from life in the game. He wills his way through the emotion, purposely pays attention to Cleopatra's small talk.

Cleopatra notices his movements, "Well one of my business associates owns this place and by request he built this little restaurant. He owes me a favor and some change, what do you think?" Michael Lee looks around, he sees the African art with its deep and vibrant colors... of red, orange, brown and sand. He also admires that every booth has rich deep leather seating. The sound system is playing smooth jazz, rather than the music upstairs, which is a nice touch.

SOBEK KHASKHEMWY MERI RA

Seeing a full bar Michael Lee asks, "How about a beer? I drink Red Stripe." Antwon returns as the smell of roasted lamb fills the room, "Dinner is served Mistress." Placing the dish of mouthwatering lamb, its artistic appearance reveals the well-preserved flavor and juices. "I know you are hungry, what would you like to eat? You can have anything you like."

Looking at Cleopatra's meal he pauses, "I would like a Ribeye prepared medium rare, garlic potatoes and some asparagus. Don't forget that Red Stripe to wash all that down." As Antwon walks away, mumbling in Xhosa. "Now that we have all the pleasantries out of the way, Montello has made his move. Two of my crew snatched one of his boys from a party. He didn't say much, so we decided to let him go to see what happens.

Soon afterwards, there was an attempt to merc one of my homies who is very close to me." Staring into Michael Lee's intense expression Cleopatra cuts into the juicy flesh of the medium rare lamb held hostage by the fork. She seductively inserts it in her mouth relishing the flavor in complete satisfaction. She gingerly picks up the wine glass, as the glass connects with her beautiful lips, she closes her eyes in ecstasy. She savors the delicious flavor as it flows over her tongue. Keeping them closed till the enjoyment of the wine excites every sense and then slowly opening her eyes.

"Michael Lee, you don't have to thank me for the dinner. I owe you for all the good work you're doing. I have full confidence in you and your people. I know it's hard for you to work with us, due to your history with other Houses of Hades Realm. That is why I am here PERSONALLY to make sure there are no misunderstandings. Therefore, I arranged this dinner where we can put everything on the table and move forward. I bet you have questions about your sister and my brother. I am here to answer what I can, but keep in mind our immediate concern is Montello Roy's alliance with Keon and Mephisto Lynx."

Michael Lee clears his throat, "Cleo, I can respect that, so I expect you to be on your game and get to the point of the matter. The questions about my sister and your brother will come after we handle these clowns who are trying to bring about the end of the world. I am going to put them out of their misery with extreme prejudice. I see the picture becoming clearer, I am in to win it. Now that I know about my sister, I am thinking your brother may have gotten my sister in some bullshit. Knowing what I know now, I want to get her out of whatever it is." The smell of the ribeye invades the conversation as Antwon places a cold Red Stripe on the table.

"Would that be all? Any steak sauce, all though this steak doesn't need it. I am sure you want a load of A-1 or something."

Michael Lees smiles, "My man, thank you for this beautiful piece of meat, it is as beautiful as your Baroness."

Antwon protests, "Do not address the Baroness as a piece of meat... sir. I will be forced to amend your behavior." Michael Lee again smiles, with an overstanding for the respect that Antwon has for Cleopatra. He himself is beginning to have the same thoughts.

"Cool your horses for a sec, I was just enjoying the look of the food. I know you don't care too much for me.

"Michael Lee winks at Cleopatra, "I see I can always count on you keeping it real with me."

We both are looking out for Cleopatra; remember I am not the enemy.

Antwon replies, "Sir, you are correct I don't care for you much, however my Baroness sees something in you."

Michael Lee snaps the cloth napkin, "I'd like to enjoy this steak and a cold beer." Michael Lee dives into the steak savoring the juices as he pulls the fork out of his mouth. Taking a long drink of the ice-cold Red Stripe, smacking his lips, "Now this is how a steak should taste, my compliments to the chef. Cleo! the food here is righteous."

Antwon before leaving takes a moment to speak his mind. "I see, you do have some sort of civilized tongue." Cleopatra chuckles as Antwon makes a grand exit at Michael Lee's expense.

CHAPTER 11

Mike is having dinner with that Cleopatra chick, man, have you seen that chick? She is hella ancient but I would still tap that ass any time of day. That chick is fine like a motherfucka." Ty slaps Cyril upside the head, "Nigga are you being for real, we are about to go to war and all that is on your small ass brain is some pussy. Look at who the fuck I am asking, I would not be surprised that you a have a tribe of children running around every side of Chi'." Cyril sitting at the kitchen table eating a slice of thin crust pizza. "You know me bruh, I'm either thinking of some pussy or some food. They always help me relax before I get into some real ass shit. Don't you get scared sometimes that you aint coming back? I know I am; this isn't the pigs or some other set, we're going to gladiate with some demons and shit. We are going to kill the things that make up nightmares, you know the stories, the shit your granny would tell when you were bad." Ty leaning back in the chair begins tying up his locs, "Yea bruh I do get scared, but damn I am not just gonna leave you and Mike hanging. My word is bond brotha, we're going to kick some ass and get Toni Ann." Cyril looks at Ty, his thoughts going back in time to 6 years ago. When they all met in Chicago's Cook County

Jail. A few members of the Gangster Disciples were having issues with Ty over some commissary. They claimed that his cousin shorted them some Ramen Noodles in agreement for some weed. Two tables away Michael Lee was sitting, reading a beaten-up copy of The Autobiography of Malcolm X. He was in Cell Block 6 for a violation of probation, lucky for him the dude he beat up pulled a knife out and cut him. For the charge of destroying private property valued over $250 which in Illinois is a felony. This was in addition to a class 4 assault; he was sentenced to a year in jail. Now with a week left, he keeps to himself to avoid trouble. The public area was the place where "business" was done and beefs were negotiated. Ty's story is being young, gifted and black while living in Chicago. He was pulled over in a car that was reported stolen, while riding with his college roommate who was black and his roommate's friends who were white. Attending Loyola University on Chicago's Northside, he was pursuing a degree in Education and Economics. Being a very active student on campus he decided to run for student council president. He was on a full scholarship to such a prestigious university, which was not appreciated by some of the faculty and students. Racist comments came first and regularly that didn't bother him at all, he overstood being black, that's to be expected. The incident that moved him was having a noose taped on his locker in the swimming pool area. He ignored this at first keeping in mind that he was the first in his family to attend college. He kept a cool head because the event was reported to the Dean. This opened him up to be involved in the Black Power movement where he attended rallies and he adopted a Pan-African mindset. He was constantly challenged by non-African students along with African students from the continent itself. He'd won the election and went out to celebrate, with his roommate and some of his friends happened to be at the same place he was. They convinced him to go to a house party in Evanston. At the party Ty had a little too much to drink, he was about to leave to catch the last train to Howard Street Station. His roommate's friend offered to give him a ride. While pulling up to the train station Chicago P.D. pulled them over and ran the plates to find out that the car was reported stolen. He was arrested along with his roommate and the roommate's friends. The police searched the car finding 3 pounds of Cannabis in the trunk. They were immediately arrested and charged with possession with intent to sell. Ty's roommate and friends made bail due to connections in high places. The saying goes "Money talks and Bullshit runs a marathon." This hit hard in this situation... in the worst way. Ty came from a low-income, single parent home, he could not afford bail and had to settle with a public defender. That's when it dawned on Ty that it was a set-up and that his roommate was a part of the scheme. Ty found this out from a friend of his who came to visit him in the county jail. His roommate was promised a job with a prestigious position and salary to help. So, he agreed to say that the weed was Ty's. The setup was organized by the candidate that Ty beat in the election. He is now a week away from being released after serving a 2-year sentence. Details of the BEEF between Ty and the street tribe goes as follows. A total of 20 Ramen noodles 10 chicken and 10 beef for 2 grams of weed. While this was going down, Ty didn't know that his cousin owed someone else 5 Ramen for another deal. After finding this out Ty had to come up with another deal, it would cost him a little more. He wanted to smooth things over before it got crazy with jail house rules. He gave up 2 packs of butter cookies and doubled the amount of Ramen that was shorted. Unfortunately, the O.G.'s wanted to make an example based on principal. Words were exchanged, one thing led to another and they were immediately jumped on. Ty and his cousin put up a good fight but they were outnumbered. Seeing this and moving without thinking, Michael Lee and Cyril jumped in. Michael Lee grabbed one of the inmates and immediately body slams him. Another inmate bear-hugged from behind, he uses a reversed head butt breaking the inmate's nose. The inmate falls to the floor and Michael Lee turns around and starts kicking the inmate each kick harder than the last. Cyril sees an inmate approaching Michael Lee from behind holding a sharpened end of a toothbrush. Cyril catches the inmate with a choke hold on the larynx and slowly chokes him out. The shank falls to the floor and Cyril kicks it away. A rush of correctional officers overwhelms all participants, slamming them to the ground and cuffing them. They were then marched to holding cells away from the general population.

"Hey man I don't know you, but I owe you more than you know it seems my cousin always gets me in some shit. Allow me to introduce myself, the name is Tyson John Mercer...Just call me Ty." With a grin and a slight smile.

"My name is Michael Lee, don't fucking call me Mikey, I hate that corny ass name." They both laugh until Cyril's high pitch voice interrupts. "Hey, both of you owe me some commissary once I get to Statesville. I saved both your funky ass lives. 'Yo Mickey! One of them clowns' asses was gonna shank you, so I handled it." Cyril's voice carries over to the guard's ear hustle.

"Hey, you shut the fuck up! Save all that talk for the officer's report." Cyril continues to annoy the officer as the other inmates watch in expectancy. They expected at any moment that Cyril is going to get his ass lit... again.

"They ain't never around when you need, they punk asses. That is why a lot of shit happens in here... that's what I hear." Cyril finally lowers his voice the best as he could to the relief of the other inmates. Ty and Michael Lee start laughing. "Man, you are going to get us in more shit than we are already in." The first six months of his sentence Ty needed to learn a few things in order to survive in jail, some of the more seasoned inmates took him under their wings. They liked his mellow energy and the confidence he had. He always kept a cool vibe about himself, he thought of the hustle as a game of chess. He knew people that did dirt, he had family that was in the game. That street life was in the blood, it called to him. Even when his Momma tried to keep him from it. He grew up in the Englewood area 69th and Racine. He went to Englewood High School on 62nd and Stewart. When he graduated his momma, sister, and him moved to the North Side and they lived off Sheridan and Pratt in Rogers Park. He was the bookworm type, a fast learner, quick on his feet and didn't mind taking risks. His SAT scores afforded him a choice of any college he could attend. The opportunity for a full scholarship was easy due to affirmative action, never mind his academic prowess. Getting out in 3 weeks he now feels that he has met some dudes going where he wants to go… in this street life. Thinking now in the present, they have become more like family. Ty shouts back, "Hey loud mouth, you say your name is Cyril? Thanks for saving me and my cousins' ass back there. I am here for another 3 weeks; I am prepping my cousin to handle business here before I leave. I see I have to tighten up on him to keep this commissary business straight. After this bullshit we are probably not going anywhere no time soon. When I leave, I am asking you to watch his back, so he won't do any dumb shit. I will make sure you get your share while you're here. When you get to Statesville, I got you, just be sure to let my cousin know your address. Starting today you, Mikey and I are going to be thick as thieves." Michael Lee snaps back

DIRTY SAINTS

"Hey man don't call me that fuckin white-boy shit!" Memories like this bring a smile as he pushes the pizza box in Cyril's direction, "Have a slice."

CHAPTER 12

Montello is giving Sheikh the business, "You fucking idiot! Are you telling me I blew all that bread on those assassins and they couldn't get the job done? Am I surrounded by a bunch of **F-U-C-K-I-N** imbeciles? I wanted both of them taken out of the picture, because if Michael Lee were to find out that I murdered his closest homies, ALL Hell will literally break loose. He is on a mission to wipe out every Fallen and human associate we have. The plan was to throw his life in chaos." Montello throws a chair and grabs one of his henchmen, "I pay all you fucking clowns too much to be fucking up. I should fucking kill you Sheikh, you are responsible for this MAJOR fuck up!" He throws the henchman across the room, "Get the fuck out of my sight, before I end all y'all!" Sheikh signals two of his crew to pick up the tossed man. Collecting himself he smooths his shirt, popping his collar and takes a deep breath. "Alright, the shit is about to start, they are onto us. So, get ready and be alert. When we are done with this Crux thing, I want Michael Lee in the ground! It's business as usual, keeping the corners and blocks moving right along. Make sure the girls are not cared and that our friends in high-places are still getting their freak on. I am on my way to go to see somebody. I am gonna say this…. if a penny is off, I am PERSONALLY gonna cut your balls off and shove them in your mouth! This is some bullshit! ONE simple task and ALL you muthafuckas choked. Some of you muthafuckas have forgotten that we are in the 'big boy' leagues, so stop acting like you are brand new. I am imagining right now that Michael Lee and Cleo are going to come at us with EVERYTHING. When you die in this game let me tell you something. That shit is on you, now everybody - GET –THE- FUCK –OUTTA –OF -MY– SIGHT!" All of the men scuffle out of sight except for Sheikh.

CHAPTER 13

"I know this may not be your style, you coming from the Southside, down here to the Near Northside. I love some of those quaint 'hole in the walls' especially that Harold's Chicken. It's funny, I bought almost everything on the menu. The chicken and ribs were excellent. That sauce was tangy, sweet and a little spicy." She winks at Michael Lee, "Just like me don't you think?" Michael Lee thinking to himself, "Oh here she goes with that flirting shit again." Continuing to flirt, Cleopatra fills her wine glass. "Michael Lee you should have a glass of wine, it's not just a woman thing. You men tend to think wine is a lady's thing. I am here to tell you that wine is a passion thing, you know what men call sex. Drink till your heart's content and see what will happen, I dare you." Michael Lee remains unphased and continues to drink from a fresh beer. "It is nice of you Cleo to treat me to dinner.... Gratitude. I didn't think you could be regular, look at us sitting down having a conversation without being extra. We have this love/hate relationship where I would love to fuck up what you have and I hate on most people you know. I know you would love to see me hanging from a pole, because deep down inside you hate that I am killing your cash flow. Yet here we sit in an alliance having an expensive meal and shooting the shit over wine and beer. I have to ask you what's the play? Why is it that you want to have peace between us? Let me make it clear, I am going to continue to kill those who want to come after me. I am going to nail Montello's ass to the wall for him tryin' to kill my friends. Most importantly I want my sister back from your brother. If anything, and I mean ANYTHING happens to her, rest assured I am gonna spill a whole lot of blood. That will include yours, ya feel me on that?" "Michael Lee that is one of the things that I admire about you, there is no fear in you. You say what you mean and mean what you say, I have an understanding of your situation more than you care to give me credit for. I will admit that I need your assistance to deal with a much bigger threat to your kind and mine. The Network has uncovered betrayal within and outside of my House as well as in Hades Realm and Atum Celestial. The network that you and your people have created is very efficient. The tenacity you have to get things done is par none; you have no problem taking out the trash."

"However, do not insult my generosity as a way of you getting to my brother, when I find him, I will let you know immediately. That is my word as a Baroness of Hannibal Guild, as a Fallen and out of respect for you." Cleopatra motions for Antwon, "Would you like another beer or blunt? We have an excellent dispensary in one of our more exclusive V.I.P. rooms. I am getting another bottle of wine. This conversation is getting a little spirited." Michael Lee resets himself from seeing Cleopatra as the enemy. He is starting to focus on the REAL enemy. The tangible conclusion is that he is not sitting at the table with the 'enemy'. The real enemy is fear of not knowing where his sister is or what she's doing. Due to the constant news reports of kidnappings on the Southside recently, the idea of human sex trafficking arises. The thought of his sister as a sex slave has created the urgency to get Toni Ann back home to the safety of their family. He is comfortable with the aura of irony, that his sister is safe… that Cleopatra knows that she is alive. Cleopatra sees the face of inner conversation.

"You really are dealing with your feelings on this alliance, I am empathizing with the TRUE struggle you are in. The struggle is with yourself; you are afraid to accept your dark side. Your concern is that you may go overboard, due to the blood lust you have." He pauses taking the last swig of the crisp tasting Pale Ale, allowing the liquid to calm his nerves.. "I have no problem admitting when I am wrong, my issue is NO trying to be right...it's to be heard. People try to read me in this constant hustle. I get a little tired of that shit, because ninety-nine percent of the time they are fucking wrong. My sister is out there and I am worried, so I get a little I touchy about that, ya feel me? I appreciate the dinner, allow me to say 'thank you' personally. I know we are here about that business of dealing with the bullshit coming our way. I will fully accept our alliance but leave my personal shit in the dark. Are you good with that?" Cleopatra sighs, "I feel you, didn't mean to get too close." Cleopatra surprised that she actually struck a nerve with Michael Lee, seeing the ONE weak spot he has. Michael Lee continues, "My sources have found out that a deal for real estate from Addison to Howard is in the works and you stand to gain major paper. It must be nice taking white folks' money, you know Cleo I can't get mad at you."

Cleopatra is surprised by Michael Lee's resourcefulness, "Keon is so vexed with me he considers me an obstacle. His goal is POWER and he is so consumed with it that I am thinking he will eventually overthrow his own father. He is such a small thinking and pathetic creature, unlike you my dear. He is aware that I possess some VERY valuable properties that are gateways into the mortal world. They are trade routes, highways that should have remained unknown to him. Key out of the way places that are very profitable." Michael Lee leans back and cracks a semi-smile.

"I thought this has something to do with you, how many damn enemies do you have? And I thought I pissed off a lot of folks. It doesn't matter I am ready for 'the get down with the get down' and put an end to the murder of innocent people."

Michael Lee leans closer, lowering his voice while looking fiercely in Cleo's eyes, "So let's kill the king." Holding her feminine, calm and regal status, Michael Lee's cold and calm delivery shook her. The purity of his darkness excites her that she feels when looking into his eyes. She wonders about the capacity of love others have for him, those whom he lets in. She watches him, imagining all the experiences that made him who he is today. This straight up street dude, with an intelligence that could have taken him to any Ivy League university. Sitting in this place surrounded by beings who want to kill him on the strength for being human.

"Real soon we are going to war with that worm Montello Roy and his Ajax clan, along with the Sheol House behind them. If you must know the Sheol House has had it in for the Hannibal Guild for centuries. Our fathers have always been in a power struggle and when I became baroness it seems to have gone to another level. Keon wants the absolute destruction of my house and he has gone to desperate measures by bringing in the likes of Montello Roy and his unsavory thugs. These are not the old ways of Hades Realm when the Royals feuded among themselves. Unlike humans we have honor; the Lords of opposing houses would duel themselves. That is to show that their power is absolute and righteous. Armies are used only by the dark council's permission when several ally lords oppose one lord. What Sheol house is doing now has to be stopped, we my dear Michael Lee are the ones who will put an end to this. Once this scrimmage is done, they will be no more, I will rule their lands and their wealth will belong to me. Their people are going to welcome change and prosperity." Michael Lee nods and smiles,

"There has to be someone else behind Keon? That's how it works, there is always a bigger and meaner rat." Cleo pours another glass of wine as Antwon returns with a new beer.

"Antwon my man this beer is on time, keep them coming, appreciate 'cha". Antwon looks at him leaving behind the bottle opener. "I will bring the beer, however sir you are going to need this to open them. Will there be anything else Sir?" Cleopatra smiles, enjoying the fact that Michael Lee isn't the 'yes men' she is used to. He talks to her without fear of consequence, even her younger brother restrains himself.

"Cleo are you worried about who is behind Keon and his old man? She smiles at him, "Worried…. PLEASE, not at all. Keon is not that damn smart, despite being Viceroy he is a moron. He is only Viceroy because of the influence his father has over some members of Dark Council. He is only doing the bidding of his father Lord Mephisto." The thought that there is more to these murders on the Belmont Rocks, first came to mind. Michael Lee leans back in the leather chair, with beer in hand.

"So, it seems that you and I have the same ideas about what the fuck is really going on. Montello is not the sharpest tool in the shed, he's a bit of a hot head. We have had our run ins quite a few times, it's the nature of this game we play. I met him three years ago when I first got these powers, he was some lackey of this cat who called himself Loverboi. Montello murc'd him while seeing him getting his dick sucked by another dude. Soon afterwards the word got out and he took over Loverboi's territory with ease. Some say that Montello paid a gay prostitute to set him up. Who knows, I wouldn't put anything past his punk ass. I do know that he is half-Human and half-Fallen, so I never underestimate his thirsty ass. He hates everyone, it doesn't matter if they are human or Fallen, old or young, he's straight up grimy. The perfect fool and tool for Keon to use. I'll have my crew ready to move, Sol, Cyril, and Ty. They are the only ones who have the mindset to go all out and get the shit done." Michael Lee is trying not to cause a scene, holding in his passion. Antwon approaches the table again.

"Mistress is everything ok, anything else this gentleman needs?" Eyeing Michael Lee, Cleo smiles. "Antwon everything is fine, no need for alarm, but please bring a couple of more beers."

Antwon complies with hesitation, "What will you be having Mistress?" She looks at her glass of wine and pushes it aside, "I am going to have one of his." Antwon walks away with a sense of indignation and asks the question, "What does the Mistress see in such a person?"

"However, you have a lot to learn about the society of The Fallen. You are a child compared to the eons that I have lived. With that in mind, I made sure to put the word out to my people to be patient … very patient. I am going to have one of my trusted commanders beside you. He's also my younger brother, so be kind to him. He has been assigned to watch you for the last couple of months."

Michael Lee leans in, "You shouldn't be talking about this here, you don't who is listening."

Cleopatra laughs, "I appreciate your concern for my safety, however I'm fine." At that moment the commander of the army of Hannibal Guild, First Knight of Hell's Gate Order, director of the infamous Network and younger brother to Cleopatra.... stands Obi Rex. Behind him in perfect sequence thirty warriors, male and female appear. Fierce, proud and ready to put in work, their aura even impresses Michael Lee. One of these formidable warriors approaches the table, she is tall with a short natural afro, dark skin and red eyes. Wearing a long form fitting bodysuit black in color, armed with two short swords on her back and around her neck is a silver symmetrical necklace. Very delicate in appearance but to the trained eye it will cut through anything. Michael Lee observes that each warrior has a different set of weapons and there were others who had none. Cleopatra touching his hand, "Like I said I'm good." The female warrior stands behind Cleopatra. "Allow me to introduce you to my brother Obi, he will help you to destroy the Ajax Clan and put a dent in Sheol House's treason." She looks at Michael Lee with an unflinching gaze. "I give you the BEST of Hannibal Guild. Montello, you can handle; but I want that dog Keon Flux for myself."

"Wow, I am impressed, you aint some 'Ms. Prissy', I see you have come to play. Cleo, I got to ask a question, can they fight?" Obi feeling highly insulted, "You doubt our Baroness? I have heard a lot about you and I want to be very clear; I am having a hard time with you being involved in our affairs. You, who kills our kind each and every chance you get."

Cleopatra interjects with authority, "You are embarrassing me, you have no decorum" Keeping the peace and showing Obi and others their view of him is correct.

"It's ok Cleo, we needed an 'ice breaker', I would rather he speak his mind. You assigned him to watch me and my crew, so let's put shit out here on the table. I like to know who the fuck I am working with. I want him to speak his peace, that makes room for me to speak mine." Michael Lee rises from the table and walks directly in the face of Obi. All the warriors' hands at the ready, the warrior standing behind Cleopatra reaches for her necklace. Cleopatra raises her hand motioning a halt, all remain still.

"Commander, right? Well I may be new to you, however bruh, you are correct in saying I am not new to killing cats like you who get on my bad side. Stop wasting my fucking time and my brain space with this rank and name crap. I rather be smoking some Kush and getting some pussy, yah dig? My sister, like your sister, means a hell of a lot to me. I will continue to kill Fallen and anyone else who comes at me and those I care about. I am going to keep killin till I get to the motherfuckas that are responsible for taking her in the FIRST place. I'll be risking not only myself, my crew and my love ones; to get at your enemies. Your enemies have been my enemies, that is how I see it. One thing I do know that you don't Commander, Keon's got a jones for your sister and he aint going to stop until he ends her. After this man, you and me can go at it all day long. I got this feeling that you will bring out more of what is running through my blood, I can respect a warrior who can hang with me in a fight." Obi looks hard and long at Michael Lee who returns the look with a smile. The silence remains, yet in a live wire second shit can pop off. Sensing the energy that is in the room Cleopatra breaks the momentum. "Boys, boys, as much as I am flattered shall we get to the business of wiping out Montello and Keon.? Is everything in place, brother? I want to send a VERY clear message to Keon, Montello and everyone else, I want them to see the results of attacking us. I don't want people to think that Michael Lee just came to do our dirty work. That would be bad form for our Guild, I want them to feel the power of our House."

Michael Lee smiles at Cleopatra, "You should come along, show me what you got. I want to see how dirty you can get or are you afraid to break a nail?" Obi shoots a menacing glare, "How dare you talk to my sister, as if you know her!"

"Ya know bruh, there is nothing stopping you, but space and opportunity. I am gonna give you plenty of that, anytime you wanna get froggy."

Cleopatra interrupts, "Michael Lee has a point maybe I should come, I am the Baroness of Hannibal Guild. What would it look like if I left all the fighting up to someone else, especially a human?" Cleopatra finishes the glass of wine, wipes the corners of her well sculpted lips. Rising from the table she stands in the middle of the two.

"It will be good for me; I could get in a little exercise and even release a little stress. Now that we have made peace it's time for us to leave brother, we need to look into some final details of our plan."

"Thanks for the dinner Baroness, I'll see you later 'Commander." Michael Lee leaves with all eyes on him. A wide smile comes across Cleopatra's face, "Michael Lee, you really know how to flatter a lady." Michael Lee shoots back, "I thought you knew."

"Why do you put up with him sister? In my opinion he is unnecessary, we can handle Montello and Keon on our own. We have the better intelligence to move with precision on Keon and Mephisto." As Obi's voice fades into a whisper, Cleopatra knows that Michael Lee is not to be taken as some common thug. She knows that he is the answer in this war, his unpredictability will be an advantage. Michael Lee is her "Ace in the hole." Cleopatra voice regains its weight, "Are you saying that I am not aware of that possibility brother? Am I not the Baroness? I know everything including your late-night rendezvous with your male companion." Obi stutters, "I am speaking as one of your officers, I am just saying proceed with caution. My intentions were not to step out of line."

CHAPTER 14

"That fool!! Montello had better not fail me! If he does, I will cut out his twisted soul and devour it in front of him! I have been funding this idiot way too long. The Ajax clan, hmp…. if we did not need them, I would have wiped them out yesterday. This vendetta against Hannibal Guild is too big of an endeavor, failure is not an option. Inside sources tell me that Cleopatra has a human doing her dirty work. Some punk with minimal power but he won't make a difference." Another voice enters the conversation; its calm and yet powerful mutes the rantings of Keon.

"Something's troubling you?" Ekon turning his attention to the painting on the wall. "This 'punk' you say, has been a SERIOUS deterrent, so far those who have challenged him have fallen into oblivion. Starting with our older brother who was the FIRST to feel Michael Lee's wrath. He is the catalyst of why Michael Lee is who he is today. Like yourself, he thought he was in control and he was not. Arrogance led to his demise, even when armed with the power of Apep's Soul. You are looking to destroy Hannibal Guild yet my brother you are looking at it from a very small perspective"

"So, what you are telling your brother is that this Michael Lee is someone to watch in the future." Lord Mephisto Lynx, enters the conversation.

"Father!! What are you doing here? Everything is going as planned." Keon's surprised expression brings a smile to Ekon's smooth chiseled reptilian face.

"Father, I see it was wrong of me to assume that Cleopatra Rex and Michael Lee were insignificant to you." Keon shoots a sharp look of indignation at Ekon. Ekon is Mephisto's most trusted advisor and youngest son. The vicious rivalry is being contained for the sake of the House's progression. "Taking on the role of being father's mouthpiece, as usual Ekon?"

Ekon positions himself in view of Lord Mephisto, "I see brother, that your thoughts are too personal for the game of power. I have great respect for the Baroness, how she rules and operates her house. She rules with the velvet voice along with a touch of an iron hand. I am wondering if you are really over her rejection of you, come on brother… really? The goal is not only to bring her family's name shame and ascertain the resources that her Guild has amassed. But most importantly to gain control of the Gateways she manages for the Dark Council. That is why brother, I am here to remind you of the full understanding of the responsibility of POWER." Lord Mephisto rises from the chair, "Keon I have one thing to say, only you can put the doubts to rest concerning this point your brother has made. Leave your feelings out of this. This Baroness... 'this female' seems to have caused you to lose your focus. Remember my son, revenge is a stumbling block on the path to power. I am leaving for France in a few days, expecting you and Ekon to have retrieved the Crux of Baal." Ekon had earned the position of counselor to Lord Mephisto, due to being in the shadows orchestrating the community of spies throughout Hades Realm. As they exit Ekon turns and sees the frustration in Keon's demeanor. The look in Keon's eyes says to Ekon, "One of these days it's you and me." As they enter the elevator Ekon is quick to make a point to Mephisto, "Father, I am concerned... very concerned that Keon's composure could lead to failure in overtaking Hannibal Guild. I will support Keon more diligently."

Knowing the ulterior motives of his son, Mephisto smiles as he turns to Ekon, "I know you will, because your ambitions are greater than Keon's, however, do not allow that ambition to cloud your judgement. At the first miscalculation you make, he is going to make sure you pay for it. So be careful, Keon is Viceroy for a reason, he has a knack for deception." Ekon marginalizes his father's words concerning his brother, continuing to vocally march forward with his critique of Keon's abilities.

"I am counting on him to slip up when it comes to Cleopatra, that way we can set up negotiations with Hannibal Guild. Once we get the Crux of Baal in our hands we will have a serious advantage in the eyes of some of the ancient houses of Hades Realm. My brother's juvenile's rantings are annoying, yet necessary action for the much bigger game. I want this entire city under Sheol House control, that is my objective." As they approach the limo, the security team takes lead. As Lord Mephisto enters the limo, Ekon internally chuckles at the thought of power for himself.

"Father, you and the rest of your fools, have no idea what's coming. I will soon rule Sheol House when all this is over." Lord Mephisto settles into the lavish leather back seat, taking the glass of bourbon from a servant already inside. The limo door closes and the limo drives off smoothly and swiftly. Seconds later, the black SUV that went unnoticed pulls off to follow.

CHAPTER 15

Michael Lee sits at the kitchen table, lost in thought as the Blues plays on radio. It's Sunday dinner at his mother's house, her home cooking is the cure for the week he has had. The smell of his mother's cooking is the remedy for a bad hangover.

"What's on your mind baby, you always seem so distant when you come visit us." Momma Leah asks over the water running in the sink as she washes the Collard Greens. "Are you hungry? I got some chicken in the fridge till the food get done, it seems like women today can't even boil water. Don't worry Baby, Momma got you."

"I'm good Ma, just got this real important matter happening real soon. You know me when the Game is on." Getting up from his chair Michael Lee opens the fridge, seeing the chicken drumsticks on a dish he grabs it with a child's anticipation. But before the door closes, he sees the ketchup, both chicken and ketchup exit the fridge together. Momma Leah elbow deep in the kitchen sink, her hands finally emerge with dripping wet collards.

"Boy don't give me that shit, you're not telling me something, I am your mother. You know how I start to worry about those streets, you aint no damn thug. You always seem to be taking on someone else's problems or taking on so much by yourself. Baby I think you spend too much time away from us, you need to visit more often." Reaching for the loaf of bread on top of the fridge, he makes himself a sandwich with the chicken and ketchup.

"Ma quit worrying about me and those streets, I know them the way you know cooking. I like to be by myself most of the time, I don't trust that many people. You know how cats are out there, I know who to talk to and who not to talk to. No need to worry so much Ma, I have folks who got my back." He smiles at his mother as she eases up a bit.

She tries not to laugh while hitting him on the shoulder with wet hands. As he pulls the chicken from the oven, making sure it's hot in the center. Momma Leah sliding in once again, "You better not be lying to me boy, you know I hate that. You know you can tell me anything and I mean anything, remember the rule is ... It's not what you say, but how you say it."

"Yea Ma, I feel you on that." Hugging his mother laughing while getting wet in the process. His momma had been his verbal punching bag during his teen-aged years, directing all his anger at the world towards her. She had a new man once in her life, Michael Lee was not a fan. This man proved himself to be a cheat and a functional dope fiend who made a mockery of Momma Leah's love. She loved this man's dirty ass draws. In addition, there were too many holidays and birthdays without his father, his father had a new family and he had a new brother. The visits with his father, his new wife, and her family just added fuel to simmering hate. He had no room for forgiveness, even going to church was not a lasting relief. It was not until one day going out on the block, he decided to forgive his mother. He felt if anything was to happen to him, he didn't want his mother to live with the guilt. Now here they are hugging and bouncing to some Blues, laughing and having a good time. He used to think he would hate his mother forever, but life has a way of having you do the things a cat wouldn't think they do.

"You are looking a little thin baby, so do any of your so-called women cook and feed you?" Walking over to the stove, he lifts the lid and dips his finger in the collard greens, taking a single leaf and eats it.

"Damn Ma, can't no chick out there burn as good as you do, ain't too many females like you around." Moving Michael Lee out of her way she pulls a wood spoon and uncovers the pot stirring the savory contents. After tasting she gives Michael Lee a spoonful of the delicious pot liquor.

"Tell me something I don't already know, baby ain't no woman out there like your Momma."

He kisses her cheek, "Ma, you must have known I was in the mood for some home cooking. I bet you gave Pop a run for his money back in the day."

Looking over her glasses, "Baby your Momma got game, I just don't tell you."

He always asks the question, "How is Pop?" She covers the pot and reaches for the kitchen towel close by and begins to wipe her hands.

"You know your father, that woman he married and her kids are probably driving him crazy. You should go and see him one of these days… he is your father."

He looks at his watch, "Momma you know he ain't thinking about me. And you know that snaggletooth bitch has Pop on a very short leash, so she can get at his money. She so worried about him giving us money and shit."

"Boy!! Watch your language in my house, you know I don't like you cussing. You can't blame your daddy for who he loves."

Michael Lee lowers his voice, still with the edge of anger. "He is a weak ass dude to let some stank ass chick come between him and his children. I know that ass can't be that good, come on Momma!" Momma Leah puts down the towel and calmly holds her angry son's hands. She feels the hurt in the emotions of his words. She wishes that he would let go of it, however she knows some things take time.

"I only have this to say, he is still your father … give him some respect." Eyes roll in the deepest space of his head, with a loud sigh, ah-ight.

"Ok Ma, that's just how I feel, I'm entitled to my feelings right?" She knows at this moment that Michael Lee is not really feeling it.

Shrugging her shoulders, she still maintains her point, "I am just saying Baby that he is your father. The Bible says, 'honor thy Mother and Father'."

Hiding his irritation Michael Lee replies, "If God is real then why didn't he help you and Pop stay together? I

101

am still pissed off; I just think you are covering for him sometimes. Like it doesn't matter how I feel, ya know?"

She hugs him, gently grabs the sides of his face, "I love you." She pulls him close and kisses him on his cheeks and catching him by surprise gives him a kiss on his lips.

"Ok, ok, okaaaay Ma, just keep praying for me." Michael Lee hugs his mother a little longer, a little tighter and he looks at her with all the love he can muster. "Ma, I know it was rough between us for a minute, but you know you and my father splitting was hard for me. I was angry at you and Pop for a minute, but now it's all good. I know you want to help, really, I am all good." Giving them both space Momma Leah steps back to promote a very important point to Michael Lee, the man. She is feeling the need to pull rank reminding her son who is the child and who is the mother.

"I am glad that we get along too, however you are scaring me a little bit. I don't know where this is coming from. Baby, you know I am always going to worry, I gave birth to you. I am that type of mother who is concerned about what affects her children. You may be the man on the street, but you are my child."
"Ma I just wanted you to know that, I know you worry about me on these streets." Looking his mother dead bang once again he smiles, then she smiles back. Now that the chain of command has been established. That the ritual between mother and son has once again been reestablished.

"Momma what can I do to help move this cooking faster, I am hungry as hell." The laughing, cooking, and music,

"Awwwwww shit !!!!!, I meant 'shoot' excuse my language." Momma Leah catches herself. "You know that this is my favorite song, she sings to the lyrics… **"Members only, it's a private Party, don't need no money to qualify…"** Momma Leah closes her eyes as she sings the lyrics.

"I know Momma, you've been reminding me since I was twelve." She sings a little more of the lyrics, smiling, her eyes closed. "Baby you remember?" She's very happy to have her son here tonight, when he was a boy, he was different from other children. The family always thought of him as "grouchy" and spoiled. Because of that she protected him, she never wanted any of her children to feel unloved. She didn't want to be like how her mother was to her, when she was growing up in the South. This moment right now, he is smiling, relaxed, whatever is on his mind, doesn't exist in this moment. She's going to enjoy this moment for as long as it lasts, the kitchen golden burnt mustard hue seems to enhance the vibe and the room has gotten a lot brighter. The antique chandelier over the kitchen and home to small wattage lights bounces to the rhythm of the music. The pictures that hold the souls of ancestors, family and friends smiling as they watch. The old school Frigidaire has been with the family, since Aunt Lillie came from the South, back in the '50's.

"Hey Momma, ya know something?" Momma Leah turns down the music. Maybe now he's ready to talk, he has relaxed a little. She sits down eye to eye and is ready to listen to her son.

"Okay baby you have Momma's attention, now tell me what is really going on." She knew that when Michael Lee wanted you to know something you had to give him your full attention. She wanted to be ready to handle whatever he had to say, wanting him so badly to tell her the whole story. All the while as Momma Leah prepares herself for what he has to say, he knows he can't tell her what's really going on…not yet. He wishes he could tell her all about those demons that she prays against, they would laugh in her face. They would tell her who really runs the block, the suburbs, downtown, and how they are running the world. She would see how they come in all races, religions, social-political and all that makes the world spin. At this moment he wanted to express REAL love to her by not lying.

"I just wanted to sit for a minute, with my Momma. Let you know how much I am enjoying hanging out with you. There are things I want to tell you, I'm not going to lie, now is not the time. I didn't want to tell you, because you do worry."
Momma Leah interrupts him, "You not going to tell me, makes me worry more, you know that? I will work thru; Jesus will help me. Whatever you are going thru he will get you through, so I'm going to put it in his hands."
Michael Lee now holds his mother's hands and nods an

'ok'. He remembers, there was this kid Marcus who fucked with him every chance he got. One day Marcus happened to see him and this time began harassing him about taking money from his mother. After he refused, Marcus threw him to the ground and began to beat on him. Marcus was so into wailing on him, he didn't see the gold Ford Pinto pull into the parking lot. Michael Lee just happened to see the car as he was trying to protect himself, he knew who and what was coming. He was resigned to taking a few punches in the face, then they suddenly stopped. All he remembers someone hurdling over him, moving at the speed of light. His mother was chasing Marcus, he remembers laying on the ground and smiling. Marcus was going to get his ass kicked by his mother so this ass whooping was worth it. That brought him such satisfaction, that's the moment when his mother became his She-roe. Momma Leah sees his eyes light up, stopping in the middle of her long-faded testimonial. The tension leaves her, the anticipation remains of what Michael Lee has to say. Michael Lee begins again, his less intense tone.

"Hey ma, relax, it's all good. You know me always overthinking shit." She interrupts, "Boy, you need to stop all that cussing, it's Sunday."

"My bad Momma you know how it is. I just wanted to tell you that I have been going thru some things, but I am maintaining. I just want you to relax and know that I love you."

Still suspicious she lets go, "I gave birth to this boy, he is not telling what he really wants to say." She is no fool, she lets him off this time.

"You are not telling what you really want to say, I understand Baby. When you're ready to tell me, I'm here. I know you have your reasons; remember I'm your mother. I just want you to be careful, those streets, it aint where I want you to be, I pray that the things you are doing will stop."

"You take it as it comes, ya feel me Ma?" A last attempt to pull the info out her son, "You still selling drugs with your uncle? My brother knows he is too damn old to be doing that shit. Both of y'all need to stop before you go back to jail for good. You know how the police is. They would shoot you before they cuff you." Catching herself she goes back to the pot of collards on the stove. "Talking about you and my baby brother almost made me burn the greens."

Michael Lee laughing, "Nah, Momma, I am too revolutionary to be selling drugs to my community...that would be hypocritical. When I heard that Sistah in California put it out there that the C.I.A. introduced crack to the Afrikan community in 1980, slinging rock ended for me. Now my beef is with these corrupt ass pigs and politicians of this city. They got the dope game sealed; nobody is or was making any money, they are taking it all. Even the Alderman is on the take, allowing police to do as they please. As for my uncle, your "baby brother" he is a little too on edge for me, the game has traumatized him.

Which is another reason, I don't associate with a lot of cats I used to. I just got hired to work security at this spot called …. The Sphere. You know that I gotta eat, when I am not eating here. I know you hate me doing that type of work, the pay is straight, plus, I am good at it."

CHAPTER 16

There's a sound of a set of keys at the front door. Michael Lee holds his composure becoming alert. A very familiar voice calls out, "Granny, where you at?" Meekin walks in talking on her cell phone, as her voice gets closer the back and forth conversation gets louder. "Listen, I am at my granny's house. I will call you when I am done and let you know I am on my way." The muffed and fuming voice from the other side of the call. "I thought you already went to your granny's house!? You said you were stopping there first... an hour ago!"

"I had to take care of some business, STOP being so damn insecure. Relax, do I ask you a million questions? Check yourself, boy you lucky I am in front of my granny, I would be cussing you out!" Stopping under the archway, she drops her purse on the wooden chair near the china cabinet still holding on to her car keys.

Her voice gets sterner and lower, "Nigga, I said I will call you when I am on my way there, DON'T! rush me.." She looks over, seeing her uncle, she smiles. "My uncle is here, remember my uncle?" Michael Lee follows her que,

"Who are you talking to and why they got my name in their mouth? Is it one of those wanksters you mess with?"

Meekin is trying not to laugh, they have played this game before. A scene from a "Bad Boys" movie, she's egging Michael Lee to speak a little louder.

"Why are you putting me in your business? I'm getting tired of having to always put shit in order. What is wrong with these youngsters today, they ain't got no goddamn damn sense!!" Momma Leah hits Michael Lee on the shoulder trying not to laugh as the conversation goes on.

She couldn't help herself from joining in, "Boy, what have I told about messing with Mimi's friends, you are going to scare them."

Michael Lee looks at her with a surprised look, "Ma, when I hear my niece coming into the house with some clown talking noise I wanna know what's cracking, do I have to flex?" Covering her mouth to keep from laughing and hitting him again,

"See what you got me doing?" Michael Lee loudly whispers.

"I get it from you, remember you got game" Meekin signals, the "ok, you can stop" look, "Don't pay attention to my uncle, say that again? I want to be sure I heard you right, so there's no confusion in what I say next." There was a good three minutes of silence, "Hold up, FIRST thing nigga, that's my uncle. He wouldn't waste his time with your cryin' ass, so on that note... good night. Say hello to YOUR friend the Vaseline. No you were not just playing, you were talking crap. One word, he'll be on you like white on rice. I wasn't going to break up with you, but now you done pissed me off, BYE!!!!!" She hangs up and takes off her coat, adjusts her clothes then gives her granny a kiss on the cheek. She acts if nothing is going on, calmly sits down with her uncle.

"Hey granny I'm hungry, what's cooking? The food smells good every time I come over and hang out with you."

Momma Leah making the last rounds of tasting the food, "I am glad that you enjoy my cooking baby, but when are you going to learn how to cook? It ain't about no man, I mean for yourself. You know that I'm not always going to be here."

"Granny you know I can get busy with work; I just don't have the time." Michael Lee interrupts with perfect comedic timing,

"You meant to say, you don't have the skills." As he takes a bite of the chicken sandwich, closing his eyes diving deep into the treat.

"What's up uncle? Heard you crying to granny about some chick you had to break up with."

"Nah, just here to hang out, you know it's been a minute. Just lettin' y'all know I'm still alive. I got a new gig at The Sphere, I'll let you in free Cuzzo, so slide thru Friday." Meekin with excitement as if she's hit the lottery,

"You got a job at The Sphere?! So, you know me and my girls are comin' to turn it up. That's where the REAL men go." Meekin grabs her phone, speedily dialing, as Michael Lee continues to talk.

"Don't come into the space with those wild ass friends of yours, thinking you can get away with acting a fool."

Meekin without a pause, "Mind ya' business, you don't really know my friends. And you of all people to talk, look at who you hang with. Let's see, your homeboy Cyril has the weakest game when talking to women. Every time that time that brotha sees me, he's trying to mack at me." Michael Lee keeps to himself the reason why Cyril is hanging around Meekin, is to keep eyes on her. Meekin is his only niece and if something was to happen to her, it would affect Momma Leah in the worst way.

"Cyril is harmless and you are like a little sister to him, he's just playing with you. As for this gig, on tha' real, I don't know any of these cats I will be working with. I don't want them to get the wrong idea about my niece, if they did it's not going to play well." Despite her uncle's opinion, Meekin continues to stand her ground. "Like I said uncle, they are just friends, we hang out, drink a little and that's it. I know this is coming from mama's disappearance and you are looking out for me. I am always aware of my surroundings, you taught me that. In the beginning mama's disappearance was really hard for me to handle, however I am getting better. I have to live my life and besides I got this feeling that she will be home soon. Don't ask me where this feeling is coming from, I just know." Michael Lee pauses, looking at the hope in his niece's eyes, does she know what is going on? Has she been investigating on her own?

So, he asks his niece, "Have you started going to church with Momma? How do you know? The 'Spirit' been telling to keep hope alive or something?"

Realizing the change in her uncle's vibe, she smiles, "No Uncle, I am like you, I follow my own instincts and I am putting my trust in YOU finding her. You have this way of making things come about, you get things done."

Touched in this moment, Michael Lee realizes his niece is stronger than he thought. Smiling in the thought, "You better believe it, I am bringing her back home …BET that."

Momma Leah is winking at Meekin, as to say, "thank you". She loved the fact that Michael Lee was laughing again and back to having a good time. In all the. tribulations that he has encountered he's somehow managed to keep his head up. Her 'mother's wit' still signals that something is going on, her thoughts are, "Whatever is going on must be bad, he is hell bent on protecting us." She is not going to ruin the moment that she is having with her son, by continuing to dig in his business. The kitchen is filled with love again.

"Boy, leave Mimi alone and take out the garbage while we set up the table." Turning towards her grown grandbaby, "I am going to teach how to cook, so you can have dinner at your apartment. I advise you to get here early next Sunday and help me prepare dinner. The first thing will be how to make cornbread from scratch. I promise that you will appreciate the meal more and learn the meaning of why it's called 'Soul Food'"

"Momma tell her stop playing with grown men, and help in the kitchen, like a woman should." Laughing out loud, Michael Lee always gets the last laugh on his niece. As he takes out the garbage he stands in the backyard and takes in the energy of his surroundings. The sounds of city trucks laying down salt followed by the city bus, he looks up and sees a clear and full moon illuminating directly on him. The presence of naked trees providing a canopy in the small backyard. This is where his mother sits and reads her Bible. At this moment, this is where he belongs with his family, having dinner and laughing together. One day they will know how much he loves them. Soon he will be able to tell the truth… the whole truth. He places the garbage bag in the can then turns to go back in. Pausing before climbing the steps, he has this feeling that he is not alone. He releases his instincts allowing them to search the backyard and ally, can't shake the feeling that there is a set of eyes watching and uninvited ears listening. They heard their laughter, the music and the conversations. The fuckin nerve whoever they are, invading the time he is sharing with his family.

He begins to gear up, then he hears his mother's voice calling, "Baby! The food is done, time to eat."

As Momma Leah calls to him, he thinks to himself, "Whoever the fuck you are, you have really fucked up. Coming to my Momma's house." He calls back to his mother, "Coming Momma, be there in a minute." He slowly walks backwards up the steps, so he can be seen. Letting them know that whoever they are, he is coming for that ass.

CHAPTER 17

Blending into the night, sits a black classic '79 Impala. "Look at this clown, he thinks he's top dawg, I can't wait to put this motherfucka in the ground. Thinking we wouldn't find out where his family is, after his boys kidnapped me. We are not as stupid as he may think we are." Rolo lights a blunt, takes a pull and passes off, "Nigga we got your card, witcha' yo bitch ass. When the rest of the crew get back from whateva they're doing in the Pope's city, we're gonna whoop - that - ass." "Man, put a freeze on that, you cannot talk shit. Mikey's boys gotta hold of you and then you got beat up by a 'Boss Bitch'. That must be embarrassing, so quit barking. Because of that I am stuck here with your dumb ass, instead of going to Italy with the fellas. Do me a favor, make yourself useful by shutting the fuck up. We are here just to see what he is doing and report back to Sheikh." Alexander playing his position as the passenger, looks at the feed on his cellphone. Rolo starts to open his mouth once again, but Alexander cuts in, "Nigga what did I just tell you? You being Fallen don't mean shit to me. Because if you open your mouth once again, I will slap the shit out of you. It feels like he knows we are here; he was looking right at us. Someone like you is not aware of the stories about this dude, he is a beast when it comes to killing cats like you. Your punk ass wouldn't last a minute being alone with this dude." Rolo's mouth is pushed by pride and it is his pride that has gotten the better of him on so many occasions, this moment is no exception.

"I am Lord Lynx's family, he felt I needed some on the ground training type shit. Straight up, I don't see why we can't just go and do what we do. Keon just needs to give the order and this fool's heart is in my belly. I am Fallen, I should be putting in work, it's time for me to get my name out here. It's not you getting stuck with me, it's me getting stuck with you and this crew on the Southside. Lucky for you, they say you are from this area, you're just a 'johnny on the spot'." Alexander, amazed with the arrogance of Rolo, doesn't give two shits about anything that was said. What he sees is just a dumb ass demon that nobody respects, not even his own family. He is considered the weakest link in the family tree.

"What you say may be true, but you heard right, I am the 'top dawg' out here and you are under my rules. I know that you are Lord Keon's family which means that my heart is on a plate if anything happens to you. What you don't know, is that I was given free range to do what I need to do to make sure nothing happens to you. I am not going to ask you again, SHUT THE FUCK UP!! and do as I say.."

Rolo snaps back to the mode of being the bitch that everyone knows he is, "Yo, you better watch how you talk to me. I'm not some low rank peon like you. All I gotta do is say a word and my family will give me your heart." Alexander's patience has been pushed almost to the collapse. Alexander speaks to Rolo in a calm and very serious tone.

"I know Keon told me to show you how shit is done on the streets. This isn't the palace, ain't no maids or servants to come running every time you have an issue. So, go ahead and tell your uncle, Lord Keon, tell him everything I do that offends you. And watch how he will laugh at you while I am kicking your motherfuckin' ass in front of him. I will be the one to eat your heart and nobody will move a finger to stop me. This is definitely the last time I am gonna tell you, shut the fuck up and buckle up. We gotta go back to the Northside, plus I am stopping to get me something to eat. I am hungry sitting here dicking around with you. Sitting here and listening to you whine like a baby has made me hungry, you should be hungry too." Rolo leans back from Alexander and pulls the seatbelt slowly across his body, while glaring at Alexander waiting for him to do the same.

"You don't have to talk to me like that, all up in my face man, I just know…" Alexander turns the key to start the car, the deep low sound of the engine propels the car out of the alley into the streets. As they pull off, in the trees a lone figure holds vigilance in the dark under the moonlight contemplating.

SOBEK KHASKHEMWY MERI RA

"This Michael Lee is a very interesting character; not all the players are out on the board yet, the Ancient Ones are correct though; these children have forgotten themselves. They have lost their way." In a blink the figure disappears, only the stars remain having been a witness to this long winter's night.

His thoughts, "This Michael Lee is a very interesting, the anger, the passion, and all that power, shrouded in such a vessel."

CHAPTER 18

The Hot Spot with the smell of pizza and other food being prepared fills the air while the patrons are impatient for the wait. The energy of the music, people sitting and drinking is at an all-time high. Families and all type of folks that make this a long-standing Italian joint on Chicago's Eastside a staple. Everybody comes here for the taste of Italy in the U. S.A.

Cyril is bitching out the ears on the other side of the call, "Just be there man, we need that on tha real tip, don't flake man. Remember y'all owe Mike for helping you with that trouble last month. I mean it Quan, don't have us looking for y'all." Ty and Cyril are sitting in front of a deep-dish pizza, Ty is already enjoying a slice

."Quan tripping on some dumb shit man, I don't even see why Mike helped them out in the first place. Now they got a short memory."

Shortly afterwards he helps himself to a slice, "We got this, so do the rest of the Brothers on the block. Quan and them, those dudes always crying about some shit." Ty grabs the cold ice-tea, taking in a long drink to wash down the spinachand marinara pizza.

"Well to be honest man I got no beef with Quan and them, they got their hands full in Chinatown with Montello's crew. A few of their family members have been found dead. How would you handle that? Quan comes thru for me, you just mad because the women in his crew won't give you play. Man, you and women. I won't tell you again, stop being so fuckin insecure, man it's embarrassing. Mike always calls you his main dude, relax."

Cyril tries to talk with a mouth full of pizza in a muffled tone, "I am too hungry to think about anything right now." He continues to chew while looking around the restaurant. As he begins surveying the whole scene, he spots his next attempted conquest.

"Look over there, do you see that thick ass Sistah with home girl? Cyril punches Ty in the shoulder that happens to be attached to an arm sling. Cyril damn near choking, points in the direction of the front counter.

"Hey dumb -ass do you see my arm in a sling?" Ty is usually not interested in Cyril's observations of women, his taste in women is not always the best. Ty looks in the direction of the counter and indeed the Sistah has a nice ass. But it's her homegirl who catches his eye. Allowing himself to be pulled by her aura, he gives in.

"Daaaaaaaamn, you ain't never lyin' I see what you mean." Cyril still holding the remnants of the deep-dish pizza, "She is why I love Black women, dawg."

"I am gonna holla at her, you can talk to her friend."
As Cyril makes his move, Ty gently reminds of the last
time that things didn't go quite his way.

"Hey man don't be talking no dumb shit and
embarrass me, like last time. You always call yourself
spitting game and it turns into The Gong Show. I was
embarrassed as fuck, that shit almost got the police called
on you." Cyril wiping his mouth with a napkin, drinks
some of the water to clear his teeth of any spinach, turns to
Ty.

"Hey man, stop bringing up unpleasant shit, it was
not my fault that she had mistaken me for someone she
talked to online. Now excuse me while I go get our dinner
guests."

Confidence has never been a problem with Cyril,
even when he "**crashes and burns**." Surprisingly he is
calm in his approach and conversation. Ty is still
expecting the usual melt down at any minute.

"Excuse me Sistah,, looking at you, I see the
universe took its time." She gives him the attention he had
hoped for, his confidence elevates.

"Yes, without a shadow of a doubt, you have that
'Badu effect'. Sistah, what is your name?" Cyril asks as
his eyes are looking for Ty. It was more to show Ty that
he got game, "I am glad that you see me as a divine
beauty." She smiles, giving reassurance to Cyril's faulty
game. He can't seem to stop looking at her beautiful dark
skin, almond shaped eyes tinted with brown and green.
Her locs form a natural black flowing fountain of hair

from the top of a yellow headwrap. He notices her coke shaped figure in a yellow dress even while she wears her winter coat. Her extra-large hoop brown wooden earrings and an array of bangles and rings on her arms and fingers. Around her neck hung a handmade copper Ankh pendant that hung a bit past her bountiful cleavage.

"My name is Asha and this is my homegirl Aziza, what is your name Brotha?"
With quick uneasiness Aziza interrupts, "Look out girl, you got another one, a so-called king with weak game.." Asha laughs, "Girl what do you want to eat?" As Aziza eyeballs Cyril with disapproval.

Asha replies, "I would like a Caesar Salad and regular ice-tea."

Aziza continues the mild heckling, "Was that a little too much for the head? Thinking of how to deal with us, huh?"

Humbled, Cyril just goes with what he knows "I'd like to invite y'all to come sit with me and my homeboy." Asha turns to look at Aziza, already seeing a look of caution in place. The obvious look of... Hell No, we don't know these niggas. Her silent reply is come on, what harm is it gonna do? The silent reluctance of conversation continues,

"Alright girl, you trust way too many people for me.." Picking up the order numbers the three go to the table. Ty, who is enjoying a slice of the deep dish pizza is shocked.

"Well I be damned; you didn't make a fool of
yourself. Greetings Queens, I apologize for any dumb shit
my boy told y'all. He's under the illusion that he got
game. You see, he doesn't encounter too many REAL
Sistahs, so I thank you for humoring him."

"Bruh, what you are doing? Trying to make me look
like I'm clown or sumthin?" Making space for the new
guests at the table. Ty continues to clown on Cyril,
breaking the ice so to speak, "I thought you did that on
your own, I'm letting our guest know that we ain't crazy
or planning to rape them."

Cyril snaps back, "They sitting here with us man,
they know that already!"

Aziza once again chimes in, "No, we don't! I
thought YOU   were crazy." Sitting down across from
Ty, looking directly face to face.

She smiles, adding insult to injury, "Plus, he is nicer
looking than you, what is your name King?" Ty smiles
back at Aziza. He is attracted to her afro puff locs, her
beautiful lips, and a voice that's sweet as honey; truth be
told it's just her entire person. Thinking to himself, 'I
don't know this woman from a hole in the wall but
DAMN, there's something about her. Can't put my finger
on it yet, this woman is gonna be my Queen.'

"I am very glad…VERY glad to meet you Sistah, I
am Ty. Short for Tyler, I don't tell many people that. I'm
thinking it's best to be honest from jump." Aziza coyly
responds, "I appreciate you telling me that, so many
dudes out here with weak ass game. I like honesty in a

man, ain't too many Brothas on that vibe." Smiling, Ty moves a little bit closer, but not too close, he didn't want to scare her. Cyril thinking to himself, 'What the fuck is happening with this?

Blurting out in an immature fashion, "Hey man, I thought you weren't going to talk to a female for a while, after your breakup last month."

Ty looking sideways at his boy, "Why are you hatin' on me, are you attempting to embarrass me? Are we gonna play tit-for-tat?"

"Tell him King." Ty looks at Aziza, saying to himself, "King, she called me King."

Cyril, seeing a smile on Ty's face, turns his attention to Aziza, "You may have my homie whipped, you ain't fooling me for a minute. You're playing with my boy just to fuck with me. Come on Ty don't fall for it." Ty speaks to the situation with Asha and Aziza bringing calm back to the space.

"He gets like this sometimes, but trust me he is a cool dude. So, please go easy on him, he can be a little too sensitive." Gently touching Aziza's shoulder, smiling into her eyes, Ty wants her to focus on him.

"Trust me I am most definitely feeling you no matter what my man says, ain't no shame in my game... Queen. Real talk, I knew the moment I first saw you; YOU are the one for me."

Without skipping a beat, Aziza responds in loving fashion. "For you, I will let him off this time."

An even more gentle voice interrupts the intimate moment, "I am Asha, nice to meet you King."
Feeling betrayed and being left out, Cyril resigns from his defense.

"You know man, I'm just lookin' out for ya. Sol and Mike need to hurry they asses up. I am tired of sitting here watching this love connection."

Ty tries to calm him, "Relax man, you getting all worked up for nothing, things will flow." Cyril maintains his cool, "I'm gonna let that slide Bruh, you are not yourself right now, being all in love and shit."

Aziza attempting to whisper, "Does he need some anger management'? I know an Elder who specializes in working with angry men."

She moves closer to Ty, the smell of Jasmine on her body fills his nostrils. This arouses him even more, so he provides the space.

She asks, "Who are Mike and Sol?"

"They are good friends of ours, they asked us to wait here for them. I am glad that I chose to stay, I would have missed you." At that moment the door opens and Sol walks in, stopping midway from the counter while talking to Shammi. She walks past him to the counter, pointing at the menu. Shortly afterwards Michael Lee walks in, looking around he spots Ty and Cyril, offering a nod in greetings and heads towards the table. He navigates around busy waitstaff, finally arriving at the table. Grabbing the juice belonging to Ty, he finishes the remaining contents.

"Thanks man I was thirsty, I'll give you mine when Shammi gets the food we ordered. I see you and Cyril have made some new friends."

"I'm Aziza and this is my girl Asha. She can be a little ditzy at times, so bear with her."

Asha interrupts with a slap on the shoulder, "Girl stop calling me ditzy, I can say how you have been throwing yourself at Ty. Nice to meet you Michael Lee, never mind Aziza, she found someone else to put up with her."

Michael Lee asks the question, "Asha you say, that's African …right?"
Asha's answer is laced with authority and knowledge, "It's Swahili which means 'Life'. It was given to me by my Queen Mother."

Michael Lee pauses then asks another question as if probing her. "You say your Queen Mother? Do you mean your grandmother gave you that name?"

"She is a little more than that, one day I will allow you to meet her and may teach you about it." Michael Lee cracks a small grin, just thinking she was not the 'regular' chick. This intrigued him even more, there was something about her eyes. She is kind, loving, and about her business.

"I might take you up on that, I am pretty busy though. Plus, y'all may not want to hang around a roughneck Brotha like me. My boys Ty and Sol are the intellectual ones, my man Cy over there is the meathead and I'm just straight up street. Apologies, my name is Michael Lee, nuthin' fancy, named after my father."

Asha smiles, "No rush, Michael Lee, patience is one of GREATEST virtues." Cyril chimes in once again as Aziza, gives her full attention to Ty.

"Bruh... give yourself some space, damn... you are looking thirsty." Aziza eases closer, ignoring Cyril.

"Let me ask you a very important question: do you want to have children? I want children with the King I fall in love with and have a beautiful life together."

Ty shaking his head in total agreement, "Of course I want children with the Queen I fall in love with and a happy life. Who doesn't want that?" Feeling the power of the moment, Ty looking at Aziza begins letting her and everyone else nearby know his intentions.

"I quit playing games with women a long time ago, not my scene. I am making up for that by doing community work in the trenches, Feel me? When stupid niggas wanna do stupid shit like hurting innocent people my friends and step in." He smiles at Aziza feeling proud of his proclamation, they both smile knowing that this is the beginning of something beautiful.

Shammi and Sol arrive with take-out in hand, "We got the food, who are the new friends?"

Cyril's sarcastic tone, "This Asha, who just gave our boy Mike a lesson in Swahili and her friend Aziza who has just told Ty she is going to have his children."

Shammi winking at Asha, "I like them already; we need more female energy in our crew." Someone checkin Michael Lee? This Sistah must not be playing.

"My name is Shammi, nice to meet a Queen who

Michael Lee doesn't scare."

As she Slaps Ty's baldhead, "You never told me you wanted babies, last month you were bitchin 'about your breakup with what's her name. Sis, you sure you want to have babies with this one?"

Aziza smiles, "Yes, after he has some training." All the women laugh, "Being around these boys, I feel like their mother at times."

She kisses Sol on the cheek who has embarrassment all over his face. Michael Lee stands up from the table, with a serious nature that catches the attention of everyone at the table.

"Alright, let's push up outta here time to put in some work." Sol Nods at Michael Lee and Shammi finishes exchanging numbers with the girls. Cyril begins his exit cracking his knuckles in anticipation. Before he leaves Ty leans down and gives Aziza a long and passionate kiss. She closes her eyes in surrender. Sol thumps him on the shoulder, he slowly breaks from her and looks intensely at her.

"Queen, next time I see you we are going to start my training, so we can work on having babies."

Cyril shouts, "Don't have me to come fetch you!" Aziza standing with hands on hips in soul sistah fashion, "watch how you talk to my king!" Asha calms her down. Relax and breath, I need you to stay calm. You are going to have babies soon, so let's begin by you staying peaceful. You want your babies spiritually blessed,

Right?" Aziza breaks away, walks over to Cyril and sternly pleads.

"I mean this, you better not let anything happen to my baby."

Answering in Cyril fashion, "Stop talking to me like I don't already know. Damn you just met us and you're giving me orders already. 'Ty and I are ride and die', my boy ain't dying no time soon.

He wants to have babies with you and he is that type of dude that keeps his promises."

Standing behind her Michael Lee assures Aziza, "Listen to my boy who stands in front of you, his word is bond. Also, as long as I'm around ain't nothing gonna happen to any of my crew…. KNOW that." Michael Lee and Cyril nod in agreement.

"Alright, let's git ghost." As they walk out the door, there are other eyes holding witness.

"I see that things are about to get interesting; this Michael Lee is turning out to be an unexpected surprise. I've never seen a human so focused and raw with his actions. He has no idea of what he has gotten himself into. And that seems to be working in his favor, looks as if I may have to get involved sooner than I expected." Once in the car before turning the key Sol pauses and looks in the rear-view mirror at Ty and Cyril.

Shammi in the middle and Michael Lee on the passenger side, Sol asks, "Y'all ready for this? We are gladiating with their 'Big Guns'. Get your mind 'frosty', anyone or thing comes at you, put them in the ground. Ty,

Cyril, and Shammi handle the grunts. Me and Sol will handle the Callers."

Cyril answers in an irritated tone, "You trying to scare us Bruh? We been rollin' with you from the gate. Nigga, we know this aint no game. Sounds like you scared."

Michael Lee laughs, "Thanks Cy, I needed to know you still got some heart."

Ty chimes in as he cocks the shotgun he got from under the front seat, "All the Homies are ready and waiting on us to get there. I don't know about you cats, but I am getting back to Aziza. She is the Queen of my dreams, she's ALL that and not to mention did you see that ass! Bruh! That girl is gonna be my wife and the mother of my sons!"

Sol being calm as always, "A very good reason to get back alive, so make this count. FIRST let's win this fight and be prepared for what's comin'. It's gonna be awhile before this is over, y'all feel me!?"

Shammi includes herself in, "I am with you Baby, Montello and the rest of his clowns won't see me coming. I have been itching to finish what I had started with Rolo." Sol speaking under the excitement of Ty. "Michael Lee do you feel that someone was watching, listening and waiting on us to come out?"

Michael Lee sighs, "Yea, I felt something, but for some reason I am not worried about that. We deal when it is time to deal, right now we got this alliance with

Cleopatra. Let's hold up the part of our agreement and see where this is gonna take us."

Cyril jumps in mid-sentence, "Who gives a fuck who's watching, I am not worrying about any mutherfuckin' thing or 'body. I am not dying today. When I die it will be in some good pussy and I haven't run up on that yet." Sol feels the intensity of Michael Lee's thoughts about his sister and Cleo's brother. The fact is that he knows she is still alive in hiding from something or somebody. Bringing an end to his mother's worry by getting Toni Ann back home.

"Hey man I know you are over there thinking about a lot of shit." Michael Lee answers back, "I'm thinking that there is something more to this battle. I want in on it, I want to know the whole story."

Sol interrupts, "Michael, when it comes to dealing with the Otherworld, there is always a bigger story. Humans are the last to know anything, so when you deal with Cleopatra proceed with caution remember she is from the Otherworld. Who knows what will happen after this alliance is over? Things can change and it will be easy for her to get us. I guess we both will know once this night is over." There's a deafening silence as they begin the drive down Lake Shore Drive.

ABOUT THE AUTHOR

The ORIGINAL Dirty Saint…. Sobek Meri Ra, born Dcon Cortes in Natchez, Mississippi, he grew-up in the unforgiving streets of South Side Chicago. A by-product of his environment, trauma at the hands of those he trusted the most. The realization that his self-destructive ways were rooted in the divorce of his parents and ensuing prior trauma was instrumental in helping Sobek realize that his anger was partly rooted in helplessness and despair.

Articulating the reasons behind his trauma was key in breaking free from the emotional shackles that had long held him hostage. This turning point allowed Sobek to embark on a journey of self-healing. African spirituality empowered him with strength, confronting his anger through the lens of childhood trauma, articulating the underlying socio-economic factors responsible for his troubled childhood and understanding the weights of a failed system. Confronting his past allowed Sobek to transcend his pain, using his pain as powerful catalyst of social change, and through storytelling by sharing powerful accounts from his trouble youth to connect with those facing the same challenges. Dirty Saints is a work that was 10 years in the making…. "GOOD GUYS", ain't always the Ones wearing white.

DIRTY SAINTS

www.ingramcontent.com/pod-product-compliance
Lightning Source LLC
Chambersburg PA
CBHW060126260626
47160CB00005B/2035